Bloodroot: 101 Dadmations

Tim Lewis Rue

authorHOUSE®

AuthorHouse™
1663 Liberty Drive
Bloomington, IN 47403
www.authorhouse.com
Phone: 1-800-839-8640

First published by AuthorHouse 12/18/2009

ISBN: 978-1-4490-3746-8 (sc)

Library of Congress Control Number: 2009910771

Printed in the United States of America
Bloomington, Indiana

This book is printed on acid-free paper.

Contents

Appendix

Cover Picture Captions

FIRST (TOP) ROW LEFT TO RIGHT

#01 Sharon – Mary Rue
#02 Habitual Suer – Jim Rue
#03 Irene Castle's Bob…Fobbed – Leonard and Mae Sellner Rue
#04 Churchgoers – Len, Jr., Beth, Jim and Tim Rue
#05 Dangling Death – Leonard Lee Rue III Holding Timber Rattlesnake

SECOND ROW

#06 Exasperation – Len, Jr., Tim and Jim Rue
#07 Callithump – Lew and Alice Dalrymple Castner's Wedding Picture, 1912
#08 Our Weekly Agenda – Jess Reed, Beth Ann and Cathy Rue
#09 My Wife Mary – Mary Jago Rue, 1981

THIRD ROW

#10 Philadelphia Urban Seminar – Cathy Rue, 2008
#11 Pappy Dalrymple's Cane-back Rocker – Benny Dalrymple and Beth Castner
#12 Kathy's Concern – Kathy Jago
#13 Blanche's Blessing – Clint and Blanche Young Hartung's Wedding Picture, 1901
#14 Daniel Lewis Rue's Eagle Court of Honor – Eagles Dan and Leonard Lee Rue III, 2007

FOURTH ROW

#15 Japanese Grenadier – Al Mease, 1945
#16 More Flowers – Beth Ann Rue
#17 Little Divil – Mary Margaret Jago
#18 Doctor Dad – Beth Ann, Cathy and Dan Rue
#19 To Bed at Ten – John and Mary Van Nimwegen Sellner, 1936

FIFTH ROW

#20 Dangling Death – Tim Rue Holding Timber Rattlesnake, 1976
#21 Father Daughter Breakfasts – Mary, Tim, Beth Ann, Cathy and Dan Rue, 2009
#22 Never Again – Uschi and Lennie Rue III
#23 Dedication Page – Mary and Tim Rue, 1981

Dedication Page – Mary and Tim Rue, 1981.

To my wife

Mary Margaret Jago Rue

Genesis 2:24 "therefore shall a man leave his father and his mother, and shall cleave unto his wife: and they shall be one flesh."

Acknowledgements

Thank you to Leonard Lee Rue III, Uschi Rue and Len Rue, Jr. for the use of family and animal pictures.

I wish to thank the Hartung family historians who have graciously shared information and researched genealogy with me: Gertrude Elizabeth Hartung Snovel Gilman, Elizabeth (Betty) C. Myers Ehasz Hartung and Marjorie Ann Souder.

Thank you is extended to G. Homer Hicks and Ainsworth M. Scott (Scotty) for the sharing of adventures.

Thank you to Rich Hurd for the inspiration to publish this book.

Thank you to Greg and Kathy Reed and their family for their friendship, guidance and support extended to our family.

I thank my immediate family: Mary Margaret Jago Rue, Catherine (Cat) Mary Rue, Elizabeth Ann (Beth Ann) Rue and Daniel (Dan) Lewis Rue for their support, suggestions, patience, love and contributions for this endeavor. Thank you is also extended to Elizabeth Castner Rue Mease, James Rue and Al Mease for their generous support.

Lastly, I wish to thank our friends and relatives that have provided support and allowed me to share these moments of their lives.

Foreword

In the early to mid 1980s I wrote poems, of various subjects, most of them were family stories. Other poems were based on stories involving friends, my perceptions, or of people and events that I heard about secondhand such as "Worms Are Biting Me!" I stopped writing when interest waned, and stored the poems away. About 17 years passed when I realized I wanted to record stories about my children; I began writing poems again, starting with "More Flowers" in 2005.

My friend Richard Hurd had published his first science fiction book, Mythosian Chronicles through AuthorHouse, which prompted me to publish my poems with the same publisher. My wife Mary stressed the need to obtain permission from the people who are written about in the poems for publication. That was a good idea I told her, and that I would start with her. I was not able to obtain a release from everyone: some had passed away, a few preferred not having their names used, others were not asked and some were unknown, which prompted name changes or not using names at all. Names were changed to protect the innocent or the guilty.

Mary described these poems as 'poetic pearls' of a prior place and time; I considered them 'snapshots' captured by the mind's camera.

Tim Lewis Rue

Bloodroot:
101
Dadmations

Ages – Jan Alawateiwisi (Charley) and Homer Hicks.

January 11, 1981

Ages

It was July nineteen sixty nine
    when Homer and I came to visit.
An old friend of Homer's we came to seek,
    to the room where he did sit.

My youthful eyes did observe
    the wrinkles of age upon the man,
small of build and dark complexioned,
    he'd lived beyond a lifespan.

Jan Alawateiwisi was his given name
    but Homer called him Charley.
Charley was born an Algonquin Indian,
    guide, chief and interpreter to parley.

Charley stoically sat viewing before him
    a black and white television screen,
of Grandmother moon and Apollo landing
    reflecting light of a lunar scene.

"That's one small step for man; one giant leap for mankind,"
    Neil Armstrong did say,
and with these mortal words expressed
    science and imagination had shown the way.

"Look now boy," said Homer to me,
    "Observe the contrast."
On the screen was present and future
    and in the chair was present and past.

And I did observe
    the differences of the ages
with time marking all
    in history's pages.

TR

3

February 13, 1981

Banzai!

On Okinawa in late June 1945, Al's regiment
    moved north in a return sweep
coming from the southern point
    checking for Japs in valley and hill steep.

8' high barbed wire was strung out before the foxholes,
    in woods out front, beyond a 20 foot clearing.
The sun shone bright that day
    as U. S. soldiers went about milling.

Three Japanese soldiers burst forth from forest cover,
    they raised the battle cry, "Banzai!"
Al felt the terror of the yell…Japs on the run
    activated grenades and prepared to die.

The grenades the Japs did toss
    as they ran into and entangled in the wire.
Into foxholes the grenades landed across,
    upon the Japs the Americans opened fire.

The grenades exploded discharging shrapnel,
    six or seven of Al's companions fell.
The suddenness of the attack created pell-mell
    of which the Americans did quell.

The attack had come only thirty feet from Al,
    the medics removed the soldiers with their injuries,
none of Al's companions suffered fatal wounds
    but in the wire slumped three suicidal Japanese.

TR

December 11, 2005

Bashing a Bush Bumper Sticker

George W. Bush won the 2000 presidential election
 with 271 electoral votes of the required 270,
Vice President Al Gore garnered 543,895 more popular votes,
 such a close election was contested hotly.

Paper ballots were recounted in some Florida counties,
 Democrats wanted to count pregnant and dimpled chad…
punch card pieces attached at four corners or not pierced,
 interpretation made people mad.

In December the US Supreme Court ruled to halt the recounts,
 of due process and equal protection none can circumvent,
Bush won Florida with 537 votes becoming the president-elect
 and Dick Cheney would be the vice president.

George W. Bush's inauguration was January 20, 2001
 and shortly after my friend Bob told me this tale,
it involved him going to Home Depot off of Route 191
 to purchase items in retail.

Bob parked his pickup truck, a car stopped nearby,
 the occupant approached him…a woman overweight.
She said that his bumper sticker made her irate
 and towards him she began to berate.

Bush and Cheney was defined by each white letter
 upon a black background on the sticker,
an American flag image adorned the upper right corner
 and it was displayed on Bob's pickup's back bumper.

Explaining that she followed Bob off the highway
 the woman had intentions to waylay,
giving him a verbal tongue lashing,
 and of the Bush bumper sticker a bashing.

The obese woman denigrated Bob, Bush and Cheney,
    including descriptive profanity,
she ignored other onlookers with apathy,
    Bob stoically stood listening quietly.

The woman's vocal attack finally abated,
    after expressing herself as a heavyset hellcat.
The two looked at each other…being silent,
    Bob then simply said, "You're fat."

Surprised…the woman exploded with unleashed fury,
    name-calling was part of her bellowing,
Bob turned and walked towards the store,
    the loud woman proceeded following.

Once Bob passed through the entrance
    he viewed the woman stopping,
she then departed while looking with a glance,
    Bob turned to do his shopping.

TR

January 28, 1981

Battle for the Apple Orchard

About 1967 on a warm autumn day at Silve's,
    neighbor brothers came to play.
Bill, Bob and Brian rode up on bicycles
    amid the September display.

The four apple trees were in an L formation,
    laden with round fruit.
A proposal for a battle of apples arose
    resulting in two teams to recruit.

We decided that sets of brothers were fair teams,
    Jim and I joined for the contest.
We gave them the upper orchard, we took the lower
    and deployed toward our posts with zest.

Jim and I positioned at the lowest tree's base,
    gathered some apples and glanced for a view.
Bob moved horizontally to the top right tree,
    Bill and Brian were a busy collecting crew.

Jim held up in each hand an apple,
    "They're holding their positions. Let's advance."
Concurring, I grabbed up a couple,
    we moved forward our offensive stance.

We crawled up through the tall grass golden yellow,
    snaking low hid our approach.
Sense of play and sunny solace was mellow,
    on their territory we did encroach.

Brian shouted…we were spotted,
    Bill and he were in a hodgepodge.
Apples came arcing in our direction
    causing Jim and I to duck and dodge.

Bob was returning with his arms full of apples.
    I rose up and threw in a hurry,
my shot struck his pile scattering the fruit,
    surprising him into a scurry.

I could see that Bob was regathering his ammo
    and I rose up to throw again.
I propelled my apple up in a high arc,
    it struck Bob on the noggin.

Bob dashed over to join his brothers
    as I rocked with laughter in the grass.
Saw Bill hurling…I ducked down,
    the apple harmlessly did pass.

Bill kept Jim and I at bay,
    up onto a limb Bob did scale,
Brian tossed up apples for Bob to catch
    and from whence Bob could assail.

Jim rose up and threw an apple.
    It struck Bob in the forehead,
he lost his balance and tumbled backwards
    …fell upon Bill like lead.

The brothers were entangled at the base of the tree,
    Jim and I thought it a hilarious sight.
Misunderstanding resulted in an angry melee,
    Jim and I rushed forward to break up the fight.

Bill and Bob huffily then headed homeward,
    Brian quietly did not long tarry,
the late afternoon sun was dropping westward
    as Jim and I watched from the field of victory.

TR

Bitten

Longitudinal stripes of red, yellow or white,
    resembling the article of clothing
that holds up silk or nylon stockings,
    contributed to the garter snakes' naming.

Each autumn in the basement of our home,
    along paved Ostrander Road,
I usually discover one or two garter snakes
    having entered to winter in our abode.

Once, I stopped at the bottom of basement steps,
    looked…a garter snake was in sight,
curled atop a box of stacked National Geographics
    just inches from my hip to the right.

If I do not come across the garter snakes
    in the autumn of the year
then their corpses are found the following spring,
    which I toss in the woods near.

In September 1993 I had returned from work
    while it was a bright, sunny day,
Cathy was seven, Beth Ann five and Dan was four,
    and were out back enjoying play.

I spotted a garter snake, about 18" long, in the basement,
    longitudinal yellowish stripes bedecked the serpent,
to pick it up carefully, over I bent,
    its peaceful removal was my intent.

Picking up the garter snake with my hands carefully,
    in my left I gripped behind the head firmly,
and in my right I held the twisting body,
    exited through the basement doors steadily.

I called out to the kids that I'd caught a snake
    realizing this as an opportunity
to provide a closer look for them to take
    and learn about the garter snakes' identity.

Bitten – Garter Snake.

Dan rushed towards the snake and I…quite quickly,
    he reached out to touch it then,
the serpent lashed in response suddenly,
    Dan's left forefinger was bitten!

The snake's teeth punctured the forefinger's flesh,
    Dan recoiled back his left hand.
Blood seeped up to the surface and dripped
    to the ground where we did stand.

The garter snake twisted its head about,
    wriggling quite skittish,
opened its mouth to bite me,
    the oral interior was whitish.

I stepped beyond Cathy, Beth Ann and Dan,
    raised both arms back and up high,
the garter snake wriggled while elevated,
    I thrust forward…letting the snake fly.

Sailing towards the woods where I had aimed,
    the snake dropped into grass and there lain.
I've told others that I gave the snake a plane ride
    …without the benefit of a plane.

Mary dabbed the wound with hydrogen peroxide,
    wrapped Dan's finger with a band aid.
Dan did not cry, but grabbing at the snake
    and being bitten…was the price to be paid.

TR

February 1, 1981

<u>Blackout by Blackflies</u>

In the early summer on sunny June 29, 1969,
    as an A.U. staff member it was my first year,
we traveled north by van on a Canadian logging road
    filled with people, supplies and camping gear.

Don parked the van next to Lac Landron's edge,
    I wondered why it was so dark.
Strange since it was late afternoon
    but realizing why the sun was gone…was stark.

A multitude of blackflies covered the windows
    in a huge, thick, dark swarm.
I gulped when I saw that I wore only shorts
    since the weather had been so warm.

It was time to unpack the van
    but I was hesitant.
I was apprehensive about the strength in numbers,
    though I had rubbed on insect repellent.

I could feel the blackflies bite
    as they swarmed over my body.
I futilely smushed them in the fight
    and my smeared flesh became bloody.

My flesh was covered with blackfly bite bumps,
    glands on my neck hardened like rock.
The nasty, little devils crawled inside my pants
    and even bit my   .

TR

December 31, 2006

Blanche's Blessing

Blanche Evelyn Young was a descendant of many
    an early Scotch-Irish, Dutch and German family
immigrating into Warren County, including Young (Jung),
    Hazlett, Vannatta, Davison, Feit, and Mackey.

Blanche was born in Roxburg, on September 24, 1883,
    to Elvira Ann Vannatta and John Hazlett Young.
At the 1897 Warren County Farmers' Fair in Belvidere,
    14-year-old Blanche first met William Clinton Hartung.

Huldah Smith Hartung, wife of George Everett, gave birth to
    William Clinton 'Clint' Hartung, on September 23, 1880,
they raised him on their hillside farm up Ramseyburg Road,
    located near the railroad town of Delaware, New Jersey.

17-year-old Clint went to that fair, held at Belvidere's park,
    with Charles Beers, a close buddy.
They met Blanche there with her friend, Ada Smith,
    Clint found Blanche appealing immediately.

Clint was attracted to Blanche, Charles to Ada,
    but Clint juxtaposed the girls' identities initially.
In confusion he thought Blanche was Ada actually,
    but correct identities were established satisfactorily.

Blanche and Ada took violin lessons together,
    they would walk to their instructor in Belvidere,
but Clint and Charles began rendezvousing with the girls,
    a horse and buggy escorted them from here to there.

Gertrude, an older sister of Blanche's, played the violin
    at the Roxburg Grange as entertainment,
but she 'squeaked and squawked' playing this instrument,
    as described by her niece Gertrude's comment.

Blanche's Blessing – Clint and Blanche Young Hartung's Wedding Picture, 1901.

Blanche, however, did not learn how to play the violin,
    but lessons with Ada allowed a chance
for them to spend time with Clint and Charles,
    which for both nurtured a budding romance.

During 1901, the year leading up to their marriage,
    Clint transported loose hay with horse and wagon,
from his folks' farm he headed south, down the Belvidere
    Phillipsburg Pike, to the city of Easton.

In Easton, stables would use the loose hay,
    to amass a grubstake Clint sought the extra pay,
when returning he'd visit Blanche for a temporary stay
    since the Young family's stone home was on the way.

In October 1901 while Blanche visited the Hartungs,
    up a steep hill Clint and she did go,
they came to stand in the middle of a pumpkin patch,
    where the cows were pastured below.

The pumpkin patch was purposely planted on that hill,
    to serve for the cows as feed.
Clint and Blanche rolled pumpkins down to the pasture,
    to satisfy the cows' dietary need.

Blanche and Clint were married by Pastor W. B. Sheldan,
    of the Presbyterian Oxford First Church at Hazen,
on December 18, 1901, witnessed by Charles and Ada,
    who also married and lived in Roxburg back when.

Blanche brought into the marriage a ewe and a cow,
    Clint came with $99 of hay money,
they rented a farm in Bridgeville, New Jersey,
    next to the Pequest, adjacent to a creamery.

They couldn't afford to sell their cow's milk to the creamery
    because they needed to buy food daily,
each day Blanche carried the milk, though pregnant,
    walked to Belvidere, 3.2 miles distant.

Blanche's Blessing – Gertrude Hartung Snovel's Wedding Picture.

Blanche sold the cow's milk at a Belvidere store,
    purchased enough food for a daily portion,
she then carried her purchases back to Bridgeville,
    daily her steps were repetition.

When Blanche's ewe gave birth to twin lambs
    then one was sold for enough money
to buy a week's groceries, thereafter buying was weekly,
    sustained by selling milk at the creamery.

In 1902, having moved to Roxburg, New Jersey,
    Blanche and Clint expanded their dairy,
with a saved $150, 12 sheep, 5 cows, and initially
    milk production was one and a half cans daily.

By 1956, Clint, along with his son Stuart, had 250 cows,
    averaged 90 cans of milk per day and
produced one eighth of Warren County milk consumed,
    as well as farming 700 acres of land.

Lew, my Pappy, worked for the Hartungs about 1910,
    Alice, my Grammy, commented on Blanche's life,
she remembered that Blanche was quite kind-hearted,
    and a very hard-working farmer's wife.

Blanche gave birth to Gilbert on September 12, 1902,
    then Jennie, George, Harry, Stuart, and lastly,
Gertrude Elizabeth Hartung was born March 28, 1921,
    at home in Roxburg, Warren County, New Jersey.

"There goes Mr. and Mrs. Snovel, Mary Catherine and
    Junior for milk," Blanche, at home, once stated.
"I first saw 'Junior' when I was about 5 years old,
    as I looked out our kitchen window," Gertrude related.

'Junior' was Ellis Raymond Snovel and Gertrude knew
    they were vacationers. "They had walked a mile to
our farm from the river," Gertrude said, and on a whim,
    "Something told me, 'I'm going to marry him'."

Gertrude wanted to go to a dance in 1945,
    but she did not have a date.
"Why don't you ask young Junior,"
    Blanche did suggestively state.

"He is epileptic, but don't let that bother you.
    He is a fine boy," Blanche added then.
Subsequently, Gertrude and Junior courted,
    and became engaged on October 25, 1947.

On the night of their engagement, Gertrude and Junior
    informed Blanche…she gave them her blessing.
Blanche was suffering from angina, a heart condition,
    and passed away the very next morning.

TR

December 31, 2006

Bloodroot

On May 11, 1976, at West Virginia Wesleyan, it was rainy,
    genetics class was attended by myself and Gary,
my friend and I also shared a class afterwards,
    with Dr. Rossbach teaching botany.

The genetics professor knew that I had
    botany class with Dr. Rossbach after his.
He brought to me an unknown plant to be identified
    by the doctor, a Harvard graduate and botany wiz.

Dr. Rossbach identified the cut plant as bloodroot,
    and said that when one cuts the stem
a red liquid looking like blood flows out,
    which is a unique characteristic for idem.

"It flowers early in the spring," added Dr. Rossbach,
    "one of the first. In rich soil is where it does grow."
Bloodroot usually has only one leaf with five to nine lobes,
    the flowers are white with centers colored yellow.

I informed the genetics professor that it's bloodroot,
    and that Dr. Rossbach provided the identity,
then he told me that the man who had cut the plant
    thought he had cut himself originally.

Later, Gary and I did further bloodroot research,
    found that Indians used it for variable extents,
it was used as paint on their faces, bodies,
    clothing and on many implements.

The juice is dangerous if taken internally,
    the source that Gary and I studied did impart,
that bloodroot causes vomiting, vertigo and
    even paralysis of the heart.

The 1976 Bicentennial and Roots by Alex Haley,
   surged my interest in history and genealogy,
I thought of this plant's uniqueness and how it would suit
   being used to name a book of family stories: Bloodroot.

TR

October 10, 1982

Bluff the Bull

Mary and I had come to the hospital
 to visit her father's father,
on an evening made somber by surroundings,
 as family began to gather.

Pop Jago was ill with cancer spreading,
 spiritually approached near
so I asked for any stories he wished to tell
 and sat near to hear.

With a pad and pen to jot notes
 I listened to Pop relate
memories drawn forward over the years,
 of details being innate.

One story centered on the Jago farm,
 dated approximately 1935,
when Pop borrowed a bull for breeding,
 awaiting for it to arrive.

The two-ton bull was restrained
 with long ropes held by four,
who guided the beast into a box stall,
 completing their delivery chore.

That same day when Pop was out front
 the milkman came on the scene,
Pop took him into the back to see
 but the bull was not to be seen.

"Don't ever let a bull out with cows
 in a field," the milkman told,
advising Pop that once a bull's bred
 no fence will ever hold.

The ropes still attached to the bull
    were moving within sight,
and they approached to witness the bull
    breeding a cow on site.

Shouting and waving Pop ran forward,
    goading the bull to gait,
chasing the beast back inside the box stall,
    Pop closed the gate.

The bull charged…
    broke doors down with bulk,
took after Pop…
    chasing with its huge hulk.

Around the barnyard the chase ensued,
    in the corner set a broomstick
but Pop could not reach it right away…
    dashing in he grabbed it quick.

Pop whirled about and countercharged
    the bull in a bluff…
the bull retreated in a huff.
    Luckily a bluff was enough!

I asked that if able to reach the bull
    would he have struck with the stick?
Pop replied incredulously that only a fool
    would hit a bull with a broomstick.

"After that we became good friends,"
    Pop emphasized,
saying he was never bothered again
    by the bull large sized.

Pop's interest turned to other tales,
    reliving one's past can be fun,
the following day Pop passed away
    on October 14, 1981.

TR

September 8, 1981

Buffleheads and Bald Eagles

In the early 1950s as Len the third does remember,
　　there occurred a scenario each November.
His observances numbered about a dozen
　　before the Delaware River became frozen.

Before the first accumulation of snow,
　　off an island named Poxono,
twenty to thirty buffleheads would alight,
　　coming south in a migratory flight.

A couple of eagles appeared after the bufflehead
　　with the little ducks arriving one day ahead.
The eagles would select an elevated perch
　　from where for prey their eyes could search.

Of the flock below an eagle would ogle
　　as Len watched from the Jersey shore.
Away from its perch flapped a bald eagle,
　　downward the predator did soar.

Spotting the eagle each bufflehead submerged
　　which befits a duck that's a diver.
Each bufflehead swam five to ten feet
　　beneath the surface of the river.

One bufflehead's path the eagle would trace,
　　flying twenty feet above the surface.
The bufflehead could swim 100 feet when
　　the need then arose for more oxygen.

To obtain air the bufflehead would emerge,
　　towards the surfacing duck the eagle lunged.
Seeing the eagle converge…
　　beneath the surface the bufflehead plunged.

Over the landscape frosted
    the scenario occurred 3…4 times repeatedly,
When the bufflehead rose exhausted
    the bald eagle dropped down immediately.

Len saw the ever-successful eagle swoop,
    from water the talons did scoop
the duck who suffered oxygen depletion,
    the flock incurred one deletion.

TR

Buffleheads and Bald Eagles – Bufflehead.

Callithump –
Lew and Alice Dalrymple Castner's Wedding Picture, 1912.

January 10, 1981

Callithump

On Christmas Eve in 1912, Lew and Alice
   took the plunge to enjoy marital bliss,
married in Belvidere's Presbyterian parsonage,
   it was a secret of a few, sealed with a kiss.

Ol' Benny Dalrymple's house became their home
   where they slumbered light as a feather.
And Lew's Dad, Casper came through the night
   with the gang all together.

A thumpin' and a poundin', a ruckus was raised
   with bangin' pots and guns a blarin',
jarrin' Ol' Benny and Lew and Alice awake
   and rapidly to a rearin'.

The occupants dressed to greet their guests,
   unwanted as they may be,
with food and drink and company
   being the silencing fee.

The gang enjoyed a grand ol' time
   and Benny sat with a glare.
And Casper saw that he had Benny's goat
   with his temper in a flare.

The gang dispersed from whence they came,
   disappearing into the night.
Casper laughed and laughed as he departed
   thinking of Ol' Benny's plight

The callithump was meant for Lew and Alice
   as you may say,
but it delighted Casper Castner
   that Ol' Benny got in the way.

TR

27

July 6, 1981

Car Pool Caper

Rising fuel prices prompted car-pooling in 1979,
    Paul rode with Barney one day.
Barney stopped at a service station to refill,
    pulled out his wallet for pay.

The station attendant approached the car,
    how much gas?…he wanted to know.
Barney stated three dollars worth,
    the station attendant said, "No."

The attendant refused to give gas for that sum,
    Barney inquired as to why.
The attendant responded, "There's a $7.00 minimum."
    All customers had to comply.

Barney claimed that he always bought gas here
    in order to persuade,
but disregarding the claim's validity there
    the attendant remained staid.

Towards the attendant Barney began to shout,
    unleashing his vexation.
Putting the car into drive Barney pulled out,
    planning to go to another station.

Pulling into line at the second station
    Barney asked Paul if he could borrow
a couple of dollars for the minimum fee,
    he'd pay Paul back on the morrow.

The gas line shrunk as Paul lent Barney money,
    they were next to be served.
The attendant said, "You have no gas cap."
    Barney became unnerved.

"That idiot took off my gas cap!"
    exclaimed Barney about the first chap.
Away from the pumps Barney drove quick,
    steering his car back into traffic.

Barney drove back to the first station,
    towards the attendant he was irate.
Paul cringed in his seat embarrassed,
    as Barney did vulgarly berate.

The gas cap was retrieved
    while Barney was acting defiant.
Barney drove off; Paul was relieved,
    watched by a silent attendant.

The second service station had another gas line,
    resulting in a wait.
Eventually Barney and Paul arrived at work
    but they arrived…late.

TR

February 22, 1981

Cause and Effect

Len the 3rd and Eileen were returning from Wonder Lake
    beneath cloud covered Mount McKinley.
Traveling they saw about eighteen grizzlies
    but a caribou bull they wished to see.

Len spotted a movement high on a hill,
    a caribou's antlers could be seen,
the bull's body was out of sight,
    here's opportunity to show Eileen.

The antlers bobbed back and forth,
    Len and Eileen donned raingear.
Wanting to see a bull caribou trot,
    climbing up they'd try to get near.

Rain did patter against their rain suits,
    up through the alpine brush they rustled.
Up top white flakes flurried about,
    upon the ground the snow settled.

Len and Eileen were 200 yards away,
    the caribou charged at them straight.
Being on an alpine hillside left them exposed
    with the caribou coming at a fast rate.

At 100 feet the caribou saw Len and Eileen;
    to its left the caribou did veer.
The caribou ran by in a fast rush,
    its actions sure did appear queer.

The caribou approached a ridge,
    came to an abrupt stop.
Len and Eileen saw the caribou turn its head
    and peer back up to the top.

Following the caribou's line of sight
    at the top a grizzly stood erect,
the caribou took off in a dash
    epitomizing cause and effect.

"Don't run...we'll walk," Len specified,
    taking Eileen's hand he did guide.
To the van Len and Eileen did backtrack,
    hoping the bear wouldn't attack.

Len glanced back from whence they came,
    two cubs appeared next to the grizzly.
Reaching the van provided security
    from grizzly and weather drizzly.

Looking for the caribou Eileen did glance
    wondering if they'd have another close up chance.
Len said, "See that dot disappearing fast?
    In minutes by Anchorage it'll be going past."

TR

January 20, 1981

CB Conflict

South from Canada,
    came Scotty and the group.
They'd gotten away from life's pressures
    in order to recoup.

A Volkswagen pulled out in front of a tractor-trailer
    causing the trucker to swerve.
The trucker's voice came over the CB set,
    "You stupid idiot…of all the nerve!"

No response returned from the Volkswagen's CB
    so Scotty picked up his mike,
"You truckers think you own the road,
    you clowns are all alike."

The trucker verbally unleashed profanity,
    aimed at the Volkswagen driver.
The trucker suggested they settle this dispute
    up ahead at a roadside diner.

Scotty responded that there would be
    only two hits for sure,
one when the trucker receives a hit,
    and one when he hits the floor.

The trucker demanded the fight again,
    in a voice full of acidity.
Scotty and the group burst with laughter,
    at the circumstances of the mistaken identity.

Scotty held back his laughter, "I can do you
    a favor. You see, I'm a preacher man.
Bring your parents to see me,
    and to marry them I'll plan."

The station jammed with hopeful spectators,
    Scotty decided that silent restraint was then wise,
hoping that the Volkswagen driver didn't stop
    where he'd get a nasty surprise.

TR

January 30, 1981

Christmas Catalogs

Via the United States Postal Service they came
    in the autumn of the year,
the long awaited arrival of Christmas catalogs
    gave a glow of inner cheer.

At Camp Pahaquarra we didn't have TV,
    my brothers and I developed our own play.
The arrival of Sears and Montgomery Wards
    enriched our evenings with each page's display.

We each vied for catalog possession
    and hoarded them for hours with our attention.
The pages with games and toys
    were most likely to spark our imagination.

Mom and Dad would state a monetary figure,
    and up to that we could spend.
We'd select from the catalogs our choices
    and off to Santa Claus they'd send.

As autumn gray became touched by frost
    we enjoyed continuing to peruse,
awaiting in anticipation for Santa on Christmas
    to deliver what we did choose.

TR

Churchgoers – Len, Jr., Beth, Jim and Tim Rue.

January 16, 1981

<u>Churchgoers</u>

Ice stretched downwards from the eaves,
    snow blanketed the landscape,
a Sunday morning at Camp Pahaquarra,
    the air cold on the nape.

The question raised that chilling 1961 morning
    was whether to go to Columbia for church lessons
at the Methodist Church down on icy River Road
    to give thanks for God's blessin's.

Jim and I stated our opinion,
    it was a hopeful "No,"
but Mom decided we'd take a chance,
    on the road she'd drive slow.

South of the Coppermine Inn, on the road so narrow
    rode Mom, Jim, Len and I,
in the light blue Rambler station wagon,
    with river and stonewall so nigh.

Wheels touched a patch of ice
    and in the road we spun twice.
the Rambler's right corner back
    hit the rock face with a whack.

The front of the car faced homeward,
    we interpreted it as a sign
to head in that direction
    with the blessings of One Divine.

TR

35

Cigar Box Size – Elizabeth H. Castner, 1925.

January 1, 2008

Cigar Box Size

Doctor Harry B. Bossard came to Lommason Glen,
    in 1925, on a medical mission,
to attend to Alice Dalrymple Castner, my Grammy,
    due to her maternity condition.

Elizabeth Hazel Castner was born about noon
    on November 1, weighing 4 pounds, one ounce.
"Today I have delivered my largest baby, and now
    the smallest." Dr. Bossard did announce.

"She is so small she could fit into a cigar box,"
    Dr. Bossard observantly uttered.
Elizabeth was familiarly called Beth, Liz, Mom or
    Grandma by people to whom in life it mattered.

Elizabeth Hazel was named after both her Mom's cousin
    Elizabeth Norton, a spinster local school teacher
at Roxburg Academy, then 6th grade at White Township,
    and Uncle Hayes, her Mom's older brother.

Elizabeth, my Mom, never weighed many pounds,
    at most between 115 and 120
while she attended Belvidere High School,
    or going through each pregnancy.

Mom carried babies like a ball up front, didn't look
    pregnant from the back, with my brothers and I,
Alice worried about Mom's strength during pregnancy with
    Len Jr. and was afraid that her daughter would die.

Mom suffered a 'bad spell' of hypoglycemia five months
    after giving birth, on August 5, 1954, to me,
she spent a week at Monroe Hospital in Stroudsburg,
    our house was cleaned by Grammy and Aunt Ginny.

Due to Mom almost dying after my birth she was
    advised to have no more children.
Following my brother Jim's birth on November 4, 1956,
    she had her tubes tied then.

As a hobby Mom has collected and kept her clothes
    over the years: coats, dresses with or without sleeves,
etcetera and because her weight never increased she
    can still wear her poodle skirt from the 1950s.

On Memorial Day 2007, Mom fell and broke her left hip,
    recuperating faster due to her dancing and exercise,
but she lost weight, dropping to 80 pounds, to stabilize
    is the goal for a spitfire of small size.

TR

Cigar Box Size – Beth and Tim Rue, 1954.

January 13, 2007

Critter's Revenge

Mary and I were married on April 16, 1981,
    I thought we had settled this matter
that I did not want any pets and that she had agreed,
    so she brought home a cat we named Critter.

Critter was a small, female, calico cat
    with white, black and orange coloration.
We discovered that Critter seemed quite smart,
    because she could follow direction.

When Critter did wrong such as scratching the table legs
    or used her claws to put small holes in a curtain,
I would set her down and lecture her about her actions,
    she never repeated them, which became certain.

The initials B.C. are established as being Before Christ,
    but for Mary and I, they also meant Before Children,
and during those first five years of our marriage,
    quite often, we spent our time nude back then.

One evening, about 1983, Mary and I, sans clothing,
    were reading in bed, she was next to me sitting,
I lay on my stomach when Critter climbed onto my back,
    laid down with her head at the top of my butt crack.

Later, I had an urge to pass wind, to Mary I explained,
    she told me to wait, so I refrained.
Mary scooted down and crouched in position,
    so she could observe Critter's reaction.

Once Mary was positioned, ready to observe,
    I released a 'silent but deadly' gas,
which caused Critter's countenance to distort,
    and across the cat's face displeasure did pass.

Suddenly, into the center of my right butt cheek
   Critter sank a single, sharp claw.
The cat dashed off the bed and out of the room,
   Mary and I did humorously guffaw.

We continued reading…later, when I heard Critter's purr
   I knew she had returned as she jumped onto the bed,
starting at my ankle, up along my body she rubbed her fur,
   then slowly moved forward beyond my head.

I casually looked up from my book to see in place
   Critter's butt right in front of my face,
a gaseous, obnoxious odor invaded my space,
   then off the bed, out of the room Critter did race,

Mary inquired about what just happened,
   I said that our cat farted in my face to avenge
the wrong perpetrated against her by me.
   Mary and I laughed over Critter's revenge.

TR

March 15, 1981

Curtains in the Sky

The full moon lit bright upon Base Camp at Lac Landron,
     on August 20, 1975,
my status as a staff man would end with the summer season,
     to take a solitary canoe trip I did contrive.

I quickly redressed while other staff men slept,
     and from the tent I crept.
I guided a canoe into the lake by its keel,
     the chilly night air I could feel.

I paddled around the sandbar, between two islands,
     by the beaver lodge I could hear no slap.
I drifted to listen…all was quiet,
     the paddle's shaft rested across my lap.

I paddled down the channel, into the lake's open expense
     following an island's peripheral contour.
Sprinkled in the firmament sparkled stars,
     a loon wailed from some far off shore.

The dark shoreline of Base Camp lay ahead,
     the northern sky was clearly in sight.
I settled into the bottom of the canoe
     and awaited for a display of northern light.

The canoe slowly drifted on the lake so still,
     there was an oncoming wintry chill.
Jupiter, as a bright ball, hung in the heavens easterly,
     lunar light dimmed the starry Milky Way, our galaxy.

A patch of light with a greenish tinge
     grew brighter attracting my attention.
Another patch of light appeared on the first's fringe,
     across the sky a line of light formed by section.

At the irregular line of light I did glance
    with the eerily tinged, subdued light that glows.
The line of light did vertically dance
    reminiscent of when a curtain billows.

Along its length the line continued to shake
    with its reflection pictured on the lake.
Jutting up and down in angles the light did start,
    curtains of light began to part.

The end of summer was in this closing curtain,
    into darkness the light did fade,
that the future lay beyond was certain,
    light returned to be displayed.

For His handiwork in the northern atmosphere
    I thanked God for sure.
Curtains in the sky did diminish in intensity,
    gripping my paddle I headed for shore.

TR

January 26, 2008

<u>Dangling Death</u>

In 1976 I began courting Mary Jago and one Saturday
      morning, on July 17, we drove through
the Delaware Water Gap and detoured north up along
      the Jersey side of the river, enjoying the scenic view.

We stopped at the Camp Pahaquarra site where I grew up,
      an ex-scout camp for the George Washington Council,
and parked on the parade ground where scouts previously
      stood and marched, in my memory…now all was still.

In the next field where signaling, crafts and the waterfront
      activities occurred, though it had been awhile,
I showed Mary a bronze casting of an axe embedded into a
      log on a circular base with numbers…it was a sundial.

About 1958 the sundial was set in place atop a circular,
      concrete base with a five or six foot diameter
and eight to ten inches high; indented in bronze were
      Roman numerals evenly spaced around the perimeter.

The angled axe handle's shadow acted as the hour hand
      on the single molded sundial cast in bronze;
with the sun shining the handle's shadow still told the time,
      but in shade it and the scouts it served were bygones.

We continued up beyond the turn of the Old Mine Road,
      parked and descended to the Van Campen Glen,
I showed Mary our ol' swim hole that Alan, Jim and I used,
      cold water flowed into the pool, we returned then.

Walking back on a soil and rocky trail along the Mill Brook
      I discovered a patch of Indian Pipe,
pointed it out to Mary, we moved across the brook to look
      underneath a pine tree…it is the shady type.

Indian Pipe, Monotropa uniflora, has a waxy, whitish color
      but turns black when old, picked or bruised,
lacking chlorophyll it can't make its own food, therefore
      takes nutrients from fungus and tree roots, I mused.

Dangling Death – Leonard Lee Rue III Holding Timber Rattlesnake.

Dangling Death – Tim Rue Holding Timber Rattlesnake, 1976.

Other names include corpse plant and ghost flower,
  Indians used it for eye lotions, colds and for a fever,
if picked Indian Pipe oozes a clear, gelatinous substance,
  we left it undisturbed, departing I took a last glance.

Mary and I drove over the steep Kittatinny Ridge,
  headed towards Blairstown on the Millbrook Road,
stopped at Dad's, naturalist Leonard Lee Rue the 3rd,
  to have lunch at his abode.

After our lunch it was time to feed his snakes,
  out of its cage Dad pulled a copperhead
and he had Mary hold onto its tail to hinder wriggling
  while he tightly gripped the viper's head.

Dad directed me to force feed the copperhead beef flavored
  Gerbers baby food in a plastic basting syringe,
I squeezed the bulb, into its throat the food was injected,
  to eat larger prey it can disconnect its mouth hinge.

In his left hand Dad gripped the copperhead's head,
  Mary held the tail, its skin the viper was ready to shed.
Of the translucent, dry skin Dad began to manually peel,
  Mary peeled the tail; it did not have a slimy feel.

Dad returned the copperhead to its cage and brought out
  a black rat snake, a nonpoisonous constrictor,
he held it out to Mary and she calmly took it to hold,
  after first being momentarily unsure.

Dad took us outside where his rattlesnakes were,
  a light colored viper and the other a dark colored one.
Dad took out the light colored rattlesnake and set it
  on the dirt driveway drenched in sun.

The light colored timber rattlesnake, Crotalus horridus,
  lay curled on the hardened driveway,
Dad applied pressure with a flat-edged snake hook
  behind the viper's head, making it stay.

Dad showed us how to pick it up, applying a hooked
  forefinger atop the head with pressure downward
while the thumb and the middle finger straddled behind
  and were on the sides pinching inward.

47

Dangling Death – Leonard Lee Rue III Holding Timber Rattlesnake.

Dad said that around the ventral side of the viper
    was where no fingers were to go
because the snake can bite through its own lower mouth
    and sink fangs into human flesh below.

Rapidly absorbed is venom ejected through each hollow fang
    connected to a venom gland by an elongated duct,
its hemotoxin affects the victim's tissues, organs and blood.
    After ingesting prey does a rattlesnake eruct?

When extracting venom from fangs draped over a rim,
    dripping into a reservoir's bottom for collection,
Dad explained that the 'milking' of a snake
    does not remove all of its poison.

Dad passed me the snake hook; I trapped its head…
    crouched down…my left hand reached out carefully…
gripped the viper's neck…dropped the hook…
    wrapped my right hand around its wiggling body.

I slowly arose upright and in fear ready to flinch,
    but with finger pressure I did tightly pinch,
the snake arched its neck, twisting in my clinch,
    holding on for 'dear life' made this a cinch.

From its triangular-shaped head I could see its fangs
    while steadying the viper's squirming body,
and knew if I faltered I'd feel poison injected pangs,
    Dad took pictures, and then I cast it away from me.

Showing us how to pick up a rattlesnake by its tail,
    Dad first placed the flat edge of the snake hook
behind the serpent's head to immobilize it against
    the ground while Mary and I did look.

Dad grabbed and straightened its tail, lifted up, released
    the head…upside-down dangling death did sway,
at arm's length he shook the rattlesnake intentionally
    so that it could not reconnect loose vertebrate.

Dad dropped the rattlesnake onto the driveway,
    handed the snake hook over to me.
He bade me to try picking the rattlesnake up,
    I held the hook in-between it and myself cautiously.

Dangling Death – Tim Rue Holding Timber Rattlesnake.

To pin the rattlesnake behind its head I did dare,
    gripped the tail and pulled it out straight with care.
I lifted the hook off its neck…of danger I was aware,
    while hoisting the viper upside-down…into the air.

Not shaking the rattlesnake enough…it twisted around
    while reconnecting its loose vertebrate,
and began curling back up on itself in rebound,
    my left leg was exposed…I tossed it away!

I moved in…repeated picking the rattlesnake upside-down,
    but after being possibly bitten I was jittery,
my movements prompted Dad to tell me it was necessary
    to steady myself so I'd be in focus for photography.

I realized that to lessen the chance of being bitten
    to keep its ventral side towards me I should.
I settled myself while shaking the viper by the tail, Dad took
    pictures…that time I handled the rattlesnake good.

Later Dad, Mary and I went for a refreshing swim,
    located below his home is a man-made pond,
once Dad left, Mary and I stayed on the dock
    kissing and hugging…with the girl I'm fond.

Leaving Dad's we drove towards Jacksonburg and Route 94,
    having headed back to Belvidere another way,
after supper Mary and I cuddled on the living room couch,
    I fell asleep in her arms…it was a satisfying day.

TR

August 1, 1981

<u>Daydreaming</u>

One afternoon upon finishing an odd job
    when I was twelve or eleven
Mrs. Mordkin reimbursed me for my work,
    I bicycled homeward then.

I waved departure to Mrs. Mordkin,
    rode out her lane on my bike,
and I was engrossed in envisioning pretty Bridget,
    a classmate that I immensely did like.

Reminiscent of pretty Aunt Ev was Bridget,
    for whom I long had a crush,
for wanting her to like me I'd fret,
    onto the highway I did then rush.

Down the steep grade I began to travel,
    I steered a wide curve,
wheels struck the loose gravel
    causing the bike to swerve.

To the bike I haplessly clung,
    against the guardrail the bike stumbled,
over the side momentum flung,
    down the embankment I tumbled

I gasped for breath upon stopping
    from where I landed on stones.
I gazed at the cloud-studded sky above,
    feeling sore but no broken bones.

While lying there I began to daydream,
    thinking of Bridget coming along,
of how nice her helping me would seem,
    she'd be my caring heart song.

I daydreamed her family was out driving,
    discovered me where I had lain.
But time elapsed with none coming along,
    reality revealed my hopes were in vain.

None were coming to provide the pity
    so I rose from where I sprawled.
I felt embarrassed due to the futility,
    up the hill I then crawled.

Hope of Bridget's appearing was foolish,
    I pulled the bike onto the road,
my carelessness made me sheepish,
    homeward I gladly rode.

The moral of this story
    whose meaning was quite curt
is to be careful when daydreaming
    or you could end up hurt.

TR

April 5, 2008

Doctor Dad

It was on a spring 1993 afternoon in our abode,
    along quiet Ostrander Road,
when during play Beth Ann, one of our children,
    fell down…a booboo resulted then.

Cathy was then 6, Beth Ann 5, Dan still 3,
    when Beth Ann's crying brought in Mary,
but to help our daughter I did declare
    that Doctor Dad was now dispensing care.

I created Doctor Dad as a booboo distraction,
    proceeded to give Beth Ann instruction
to lie down upon the living room floor
    and undergo examination by the good doctor.

Weepy-eyed Beth Ann lay down on her back
    upon the carpet colored golden-yellow.
It was necessary to check each extremity I verbalized,
    expounding on how the examination would go.

I started by raising Beth Ann's right leg slowly up,
    visually inspected while her foot I did cup,
the underside of her right knee I lightly tickled,
    as a result Beth Ann giggled.

I checked Beth Ann's right sole by tickling,
    her laughter replaced any sorrowful tear,
but she thrashed about with flailing arms and legs,
    and to assist as a nurse Cathy did volunteer.

Declaring that Beth Ann's right leg was good,
    now to check the left I said I should.
Nurse Cathy held her sister's right leg in place
    so I wouldn't be kicked in the face.

After examining Beth Ann's left knee and foot,
    I raised up her right arm,
tickled the inside of her elbow and underarm…
    medicinal laughter worked its charm.

Doctor Dad – Beth Ann, Cathy and Dan Rue.

Upon examining Beth Ann's left arm with tickles,
    Cathy held down her sister's ankles.
I had Beth Ann rotate her head in order to check,
    then I extended fingers towards her neck.

Tickling Beth Ann's neck caused her to squeal
    outwardly her laughter did loudly peal.
I announced that her neck was okay, and did kneel
    near her belly...how did it feel?

Exploring...I lightly poked her belly with my finger
    to verify that there was nothing the matter,
tickling with both hands made her stomach quiver,
    the room filled with her laughter.

Stamping approval my fist slowly rested onto her belly,
    I publicly certified that Beth Ann was now A-Okay.
Cathy claimed having a booboo also and needed
    Doctor Dad...onto the carpet she did lay.

Doctor Dad repeated the same tickling routine,
    declared that Cathy was A-Okay ultimately.
Dan discovered that he also had a booboo...suddenly,
    Doctor Dad examined each patient equally.

After Dan's examination each child wanted another turn...
    until satisfied, then to their playing they did return.
Doctor Dad dispensed his medicine the next few years
    and eased away many booboo tears.

As our children approached puberty,
    physically and emotionally they outgrew Doctor Dad.
I understood and reluctantly retired Doctor Dad...sadly
    acknowledged that he was a passing fad.

TR

March 5, 1981

Drink of Blood

Len Rue 3rd traveled in 1968 to eastern Africa
    hoping to obtain many a good photo,
he visited the Mazai in Tanzania
    living on the grasslands within an extinct volcano.

Mazai are grassland native cattlemen,
    milk products are the bulk of their diet,
but occasionally they enjoy drinking a bull's blood,
    around its neck they'd tie a tourniquet.

Within seconds the jugular vein swelled,
    a native aimed a round tipped arrow
supported in a bow at a distance of a foot,
    within the 10 mile diameter crater of Ngorongoro.

The arrow struck the vein in a flash,
    bouncing back the tip left a gash,
from the wound blood did squirt
    under pressure due to the neck girt.

As the blood from the bull's neck poured,
    a native caught the stream in a gourd.
Len declined when the Mazai offered him a drink,
    it's appeal was beyond his appetite's brink.

A native took some grass and did twist,
    pushed it into the bull's wound as a plug.
Of the gourd to their lips the natives did hoist
    but not one did a chug-a-lug?

TR

December 29, 2006

Droplets of Water

It had rained the night before but the storm moved away
    on one late spring Sunday morning in 1993,
when my family attended a local Baptist church,
    including Dan, our blond-haired son still three.

After the service a deacon and I went to the parking lot,
    to converse in the upper section we found a spot,
across the asphalt sporadic puddles did blot,
    a big one was in the lower section within eyeshot.

Josie, the pastor's five-year-old, precocious daughter,
    in a pretty, pink, party dress she was attired,
was riding around the parking lot on her big tricycle,
    with plastic wheels, it was light blue and pink colored.

Josie stopped in the lower lot where she deployed,
    as Dan came outside, she was poised,
he stepped away from the front doors of the church.
    Suddenly…forward the big tricycle did lurch.

Josie began peddling her plastic tricycle fast,
    aimed for Dan with malicious intent?
The large, front, plastic, wheel struck Dan on the left leg,
    sent him sprawling onto the pavement.

Josie peddled further on and circled around in an arc,
    Dan picked himself up off of the asphalt,
he ran to the lower lot to stand next to the large puddle,
    she began peddling towards him for a second assault.

Josie bore down at Dan with determination,
    he stood waiting for her beside the puddle.
As she peddled in close for the 'kill',
    suddenly, Dan jumped into the puddle's middle.

Dan jumped up and down…up and down…repetitively,
   splashing Josie…soaking wet,
up and down…up and down…up and down,
   then off he ran to play, ending his vignette.

Josie spotted me standing next to the deacon,
   peddled over to me looking upset,
in a wet dress, with water dripping from her hair,
   she whined, "Mr. Rue, Danny got me all wet."

Droplets of water dribbled off of her up turned nose,
   I addressed Josie, "Yes, and I saw that you
ran Dan over and knocked him down on purpose.
   And then you tried to do it again," I did construe.

Josie realized that she was getting no sympathy
   from me…and looked bemusedly,
watched her departure as she peddled away dejectedly,
   the deacon, wryly smiling, and I gazed on amusedly.

TR

May 28, 2007

Exasperation

Charged by a massive bull elephant,
    chased by a lumbering rhinoceros,
pursued by a spitting King Cobra,
    wildlife photography can be dangerous.

Traveling to places far or close to home,
    of wildlife in order to find,
a photographer may wait for hours or days
    for the right picture in a blind.

Once the most published world-wide wildlife photographer
    my Dad has journeyed to every continent,
he is a naturalist and author of over thirty books
    full of wildlife informational content.

Family pictures…Dad disliked taking these the most
    during his career photographic
and would voice discontent with resultant exasperation
    due to many a brotherly antic.

Snow covered the landscape prior to Christmas 1961,
    where my family lived at Camp Pahaquarra,
and a Christmas card picture of my brothers and I
    Dad wanted to take with his camera.

Dad was the camp ranger at this Boy Scout camp,
    located north of the Delaware Water Gap,
when my brother Len was 13, I was 7, Jim 5,
    a winter picture scene Dad wished to snap.

To pose us on our toboggan Dad was keen,
    on the snow white and clean,
he wanted the surface unmarred and pristine,
    Mom stood by witnessing this unfolding scene.

Our toboggan, with wooden slats that curved at the front,
    was cushioned with green plastic padding,
and with no runners the bottom ran on the snow,
    this meant for downhill coasting.

Beside our driveway was the small hill to be used,
    with no trees and draped by pristine snow,
it was located between our house and the lodge
    used for the Order of the Arrow.

Len positioned and held onto the toboggan's back end,
    Jim slid on first to the front carefully,
I placed myself on the padding behind Jim,
    Len moved into position behind me.

As Dad prepared to take the picture
    I decided to flip Jim over the toboggan's front,
slid my hands under his bottom to thrust up…tossed
    …instead Jim fell off to the right in my stunt.

Jim's body marred the snow on the right side,
    I was yelled at for my behavior,
Dad told us to move further over on the hill,
    to set up for a second picture.

Upon finishing our setup I made a decision
    to try tossing Jim again…moved in repetition,
but Len began grabbing at me as prevention,
    I fell into snow, pulling Jim with me in reaction.

In our direction there came verbal chastisement,
    but I was enjoying the excitement,
rose up and brushed off the snow to avoid a chill,
    over we moved to the left, along the hill.

I thought it would be funny to help cause
    the toboggan to slide down the hill,
if Len noticed he'd get me…so I wriggled
    my bottom slightly…the toboggan stayed still.

Dad was again ready; we were posed and poised,
    for a second time I began wiggling,
but the toboggan didn't budge much
    so I gave up my slight jiggling.

Surprisingly…suddenly the toboggan descended down,
    departing beyond Dad's picture frame,
since I wasn't wriggling my butt right before
    I didn't think I could accept the blame.

Exasperation – Len, Jr., Tim and Jim Rue.

At the hill's bottom we climbed off,
    Len pulled the toboggan back up on the driveway,
we moved further to the left on the hill,
    frustrated…Dad had his say.

We were running out of open hill space
    …and in exasperation Dad explained why,
due to our antics for taking this picture
    he'd give it only one last try.

Since this was our last picture chance
    I decided to behave,
we setup without a mishap and posed
    with a smile and a wave.

As a naturalist, author and wildlife photographer
    Dad has received well earned laurels,
he deserved one for this picture…despite exasperation,
    don't we look like little angels?

TR

April 18, 2009

<u>Father Daughter Breakfasts</u>

As young children Cathy, Beth Ann, Dan
    and I spent more quality time together,
the memories of these interactions are etched
    fondly into my mind forever.

Spreading out our sleeping bags as mattresses
    in the living room before the TV
we'd watch our favorite VHS tapes repeatedly,
    often the most recent release from Disney.

All three climbed on my prostrate back when wrestling,
    while I lay on my stomach on the floor,
then I'd rise to a doggy position as they'd grab
    my arms or legs to knock me over some more.

Our children would ride on my back playing 'horsey'
    Dan in front, then Beth Ann, in back rode Cathy.
I would crawl around the living room and hall,
    moving carefully so they would not fall.

The kids would wrap their arms and legs
    around my legs while sitting on my feet,
I'd move one weighted down foot at a time walking
    back and forth in the hall as a mutual treat.

Ecclesiastes 3:5 states "a time to embrace" which
    we did, but as the children became older
the time I spent with each of them differentiated
    gradually based on their gender.

I spent more time in activities with Dan
    such as coaching for Lower Mount Bethel soccer,
and after he joined Troop 14 in Stone Church I became
    a merit badge counselor and assistant scout leader.

While Mary helped coach our girls in softball
    I often assisted as a scorekeeper gladly,
but to me events like 'shopping' has to have a purpose,
    for the ladies it is in and of itself an activity.

Concern over losing communication with my daughters
    and of the uneven quality time contrasts
I sought to reestablish relationships with them concocting
    the concept of Father Daughter Breakfasts.

Both girls attended Bangor High School when we started
    the Father Daughter Breakfasts in the spring of 2001,
Cathy was fifteen and Beth Ann was turning fourteen
    as we began this one-on-one interaction.

I started by taking Cathy first since she's the eldest,
    we were bedecked in our Sunday best,
the following month I took Beth Ann for her turn,
    to be fair by interchanging monthly was my concern.

I picked Sundays before church to go with each lass,
    being dressed up added a touch of class,
we departed our Lower Mount Bethel home on our jaunt,
    drove to a small Belvidere, New Jersey restaurant.

A private side table we always tried to access
    and then placed our order with a waitress.
Saying a prayer of thanks, I asked the Lord to bless,
    we would settle in for topics to address.

Since this was their time to express any concern
    and was my special opportunity to learn
I tried to refrain from leading off on a topic
    while awaiting whatever issue they would pick.

They told me of what was in their heart and mind:
    school, boys, friends, boyfriends, sisters, family,
of frustrations, accomplishments, wishes to find
    hope, and happiness in a future with opportunity.

They expressed their unique perspectives in conversation
    and I tactfully questioned to extract more information
avoiding negative judgment when making an observation
    while hopefully offering any constructive opinion.

Cathy and Beth Ann worked away from home
    at summer camps which limited their availability
and the autumn's advent curtailed the breakfasts
    due to school and other increased activity.

At first the girls were snack shop workers while Dan
worked in the kitchen during the summer
at New Life Island, a Christian camp located near
Frenchtown, on an island in the Delaware River.

All three also worked at Camp Marcella in Morris County,
a camp for blind and disabled children,
Cathy and Beth Ann were counselors, then on the
program staff while Dan worked in their kitchen.

Once the sun's warmth melts away the winter season
up rises tubular or nearly flat leaves of the wild onion,
and with inclement weather receding we now had reason
to return to the Father Daughter Breakfast occasion.

Once Cathy and Beth Ann were busy in college
and our displacement by the house fire in 2007,
then injuries, Cathy's Lyme disease, five car accidents,
led to Father Daughter Breakfasts being forgotten.

In spring 2008, Beth Ann told Mary who then told me
that Beth Ann missed the breakfasts, unexpectedly
I'd assumed that the girls had outgrown them…ergo
I was glad and off to Belvidere we'd go.

Adorned with a hairstyle and dressed reminiscent to me
of actress Veronica Lake or a 1940s fashion model
I was suddenly aware of a difference with Beth Ann
as she spoke of issues to tell.

Gone was the little girl, the adolescent, the teen…
those times included trials but blessings bountiful,
before me with her confident presence and personality
sat a mature, young woman…Beth Ann's beautiful!

After breakfast on a street in Belvidere I told Beth Ann
what a beautiful young lady she'd become,
afterwards she told Mary excitedly of being pleased,
her appreciation and happiness to me was welcome.

Beth Ann and three friends had taken a road trip
down south and previously Mary and I did state
to not go to New Orleans because of Hurricane Katrina
and our concern over a higher crime rate.

Father Daughter Breakfasts –
Mary, Tim, Beth Ann, Cathy and Dan Rue, 2009.

Over breakfast Beth Ann admitted she did not heed
    our warning and they visited New Orleans indeed,
in the French Quarter a European style was observed,
    at a Bourbon Street restaurant they were served.

As Beth Ann told of her southern tale I requested
    for her to write her story as I did wish with relish
to include her account as an appendix in a poetry book,
    she agreed, which I plan to eventually publish.

My most recent Father Daughter Breakfast was with
    Beth Ann on March 11, 2009, a Wednesday,
she was on Spring Break from Temple University,
    I had scheduled from work a personal day.

Excitedly telling me about her March twelfth birthday
    on the morrow when she will turn twenty-one
and looking forward to an improved social life
    Beth Ann anticipates more freedom with her fun.

Beth Ann, in the honor society, expressed emphatically
    about how very smart is her sister Cathy
who has maintained a 4.0 GPA at Kutztown University
    while studying to be a teacher for the elementary.

The Father Daughter Breakfasts that we share are
    the closest she ever feels to me Beth Ann confessed,
no other venue matches this one-on-one setting,
    my young ladies and I have been blessed.

I approached Dan about our first Father Son Breakfast,
    to continue with all our children is my intent,
for while our fragile mortal existence requires repast
    we are in 2 Corinthians 4:17, "but for a moment."

TR

January 18, 2006

First Pheasant

Back in 1965 when I reached the age of eleven
    I'd be going hunting once the season had begun,
with my Dad, his friends and my older brother Len,
    each of us armed with a shotgun.

We hunted within the realm of Coventry Hunting Club
    in old Pahaquarry Township, the County of Warren,
between the Delaware River and the Kittatinny Ridge,
    for the hunting club my Dad was a game warden.

Our family was fed on pheasant and venison,
    available during each hunting season,
and a small game maxim of my father's that was explicit
    stated, "If you kill it, you clean it."

My first hunting day Dad drove past the Uporsky home,
    parked near a gate leading into a field,
met two of Dad's friends and donned our hunting vests,
    the shotgun I did carefully wield.

Dad, his two friends, Len and I spread out in a line,
    beyond the farmer's gate.
We traversed northward across the open fields
    at a slow, steady gait.

We stepped forth from a field into an area
    with sparse underbrush for a second growth forest,
on an embankment overlooking the Delaware River
    sat the Hankin-Howell summer home off to the west.

At a short intermediate distance slightly off to the northwest
    an unused baseball backstop was an unusual display,
built of telephone poles and wire mesh backing,
    small trees grew within the forgotten field of play.

First Pheasant – Tim Rue's First Pheasant.

Just to the north of our current position
    the undergrowth of the forest did somewhat thicken,
there Dad would point out an elevated browse line on trees
    where during previous winters hungry deer had eaten.

I was alerted that someone had made a discovery,
    we congregated together so all could see,
a pheasant was nestled, facing left, at the base of a tree
    despite our presence it demonstrated immobility.

Displayed was a greenish iridescent head with a yellow beak,
    a white neck ring and a blood red patch adorned its cheek,
the mottled brown body was followed by its 22-inch long tail,
    vibrant coloration indicated this pheasant was a male.

The five of us stood gazing in a huddle,
    I wondered why the ring-necked pheasant did not flee,
my Dad beckoned me into the middle,
    indicating it would be an easy first shot for me.

I knew food for the table denoted practicality
    but shooting a sitting pheasant was not sporting to me,
hoping he'd be disturbed…and fly or run,
    if he moved I was poised with my gun.

To slay the immobile pheasant I hesitated,
    of my Dad's urgings I attempted to verbally refute,
but detected that my father was becoming exasperated
    when he ordered me to, "Shoot!"

I fired…between the bird and I…looked with astound
    as the pheasant flew up from the ground,
immediately…the others' guns rose up all around,
    discharged near my ears as a roaring sound.

When I looked up…downward feathers fluttered,
    an easy kill I obviously muddled.
The pheasant was now a shot riddled carcass
    which my father picked up from the grass.

Wanting nothing to do with this pheasant I tried to protest
but Dad put the dead bird in a pouch of my vest.
I did not get another chance at a shot that day,
waiting to redeem myself caused me some dismay.

Dad cleaned the shot riddled bird for me…thankfully,
salvaging any meat that remained actually.
I reflected that the experience with my first pheasant
could have been…somewhat more pleasant.

TR

February 21, 1981

<u>Fishing for Sunnies</u>

Jim and I decided to go fishing one summer morning
    about 1966, in the small pond at Silve's.
We sat ourselves down on our wooden dock
    planning to catch some sunnies.

We attached fishline to our bamboo poles,
    Mom gave us bread for bait.
We rolled the bread into balls and set them on our hooks,
    attempting to alter fishes' fate.

Jim fished off one side, I the other,
    submerging each line's tip.
We basked in the late morning's warmth,
    suddenly Jim's line took a dip.

Caught on the line a sunfish shook,
    Jim freed its mouth from the hook.
Tossing the fish back it did flip-flop,
    reentered its watery domain with a plop.

Within minutes Jim's line again went taut,
    revealing that another sunny was caught.
I impatiently made my line to jiggle
    but I nary got a nibble.

Jim proceeded to catch more,
    apparently his side was best
to catch the sunnies we both sought,
    so to exchange sides I did suggest.

To exchange sides Jim did agree,
    it was quite brotherly.
I changed my bait to help me lure,
    now I'd catch a fish for sure.

Eyeing my bait a fish did look,
    but it was Jim's baited hook one took.
Soon afterwards Jim did catch another,
    the hungry fish moved from this side to the other?

I convinced Jim to switch places again
    and settled down with a wish,
I cast my line into the pond
    hoping to catch one little sunfish.

A sunny snagged on Jim's hook,
    he pulled the fish from the water with a pluck.
I didn't understand the circumstances,
    was it ability or just plain luck?

At this time I was quite agitated
    and despite charity shown by Jim
an unfulfilled fleeting thought crossed my mind
    to throw him in for a swim.

Mom called us in for lunch,
    it was a reprieve from frustration.
A fisherman I sure wasn't
    with no patience for the exasperation.

TR

Gap's Grandeur – Delaware Water Gap.

December 23, 2005

Gap's Grandeur

On October 28, 2005 I did testing for a vaccine,
    working as a lab tech in Swiftwater at Sanofi Pasteur,
then drove eastward on Route 80 under a sunny scene
    and came upon the Delaware Water Gap's grandeur.

Imagining geologically a dam that was breached,
    forging a gap through the Kittatinny Ridge,
with a wide, slow moving river flowing…which I reached
    by my driving in traffic towards the toll bridge.

As I drove over the Delaware
    the autumn sun set the gap emblazed,
at trees draped in red, greens and yellow I was aware
    of colors setting the scenery ablazed.

The colors bedecked the steep slopes of Kittatinny,
    on Pennsylvania's side loomed Mt Minsi,
following Route 80's curving left in New Jersey
    revealed Indian Head perched atop Mt. Tammany.

From the perch Indian Head peered right and skyward looked,
    with a protruding proboscis prominently hooked.
As Route 80 curved underneath and to the right
    Indian Head above disappeared from sight.

That weekend clocks fell back to Standard Time,
    driving through the gap on Monday, the sun was low,
while the very top of Mt Tammany was still sunny
    the rest of the gap was masked in Mt. Minsi's shadow.

On December 22, 2005 as I drove through the gap's scene
    of snow patches, leafless trees and darkened evergreen,
I appreciated the Delaware Water Gap's formation
    and the grandeur of God's creation.

TR

March 19, 1981

Getting Even

Lew had an Uncle Andrew and an Aunt Dora,
    they were farmers by trade.
Uncle Andrew was heavyset and Aunt Dora was petite,
    opposites they were made.

One evening after chores were completed
    they lay together in bed.
Uncle Andrew's proclivity for passing wind arose,
    he gripped Aunt Dora's head.

Uncle Andrew stuck her head under the blankets,
    with strength within his wide girth.
Aunt Dora struggled helplessly to be free,
    Uncle Andrew reacted with mirth.

Aunt Dora was determined to get even,
    she'd await her opportunity.
She'd do it when her husband wasn't suspecting,
    perhaps involved in some farming activity.

One day it was time to feed the pigs,
    Uncle Andrew headed for the swill barrel.
The wooden barrel contained food scraps, cornmeal
    and water…around it lingered a strong smell.

Uncle Andrew found the swill barrel nearly empty,
    into the barrel…over he bent.
As he scraped the bottom with a pail Aunt Dora saw,
    and for getting even she could vent.

Aunt Dora approached with a paling,
    gave Uncle Andrew's upended rear a whaling.
The sudden attack caused Uncle Andrew to slip,
    into the swill barrel he did dip.

TR

March 6, 1981

Grackles in a Pine Grove

Belvidere Explorers went to Homer's farm
    to camp out amongst the pines.
We ascended through a meadow and along a fence row,
    trekking through Homer's property confines.

A campfire lit the night and roasted aluminum wrapped potatoes
    with venison and vegetables impaled on a shish kabob.
The night was clear with many stars,
    fellowship allowed us to hobnob.

In the crisp night air I undressed to retire,
    crawled in my sleeping bag.
I lay stargazing as coals glowed in the campfire,
    the conversation eventually did lag.

I awakened to quiet and subdued morning light
    wondering why of sunshine something did shroud.
My companions still slept in their sleeping bags
    when amongst the treetops some noise became loud.

Shapes fluttered and hovered as I did stare,
    a flock of calling birds did rend the air.
My fellow explorers were abruptly awakened by the cackles,
    caused by the black shapes of roosting grackles.

The grackles' calling gave us all a boost,
    they had flown in during the night to roost.
The whole flock awakened to create an uproaring,
    then they began to fly off into the morning.

Within minutes the treetops were empty
as the grackles migrated as a flock.
The grackles' cackling aids them in their travels
and it served <u>all</u> as an efficient alarm clock.

TR

Green Tomatoes – Beth, Alice and Lew Castner.

August 15, 1982

Green Tomatoes

Up along the shady Lommason Glen,
    at home near Summerfield,
Lew Castner annually planted a garden,
    nurturing nature to yield.

Beth recalls her Dad at his toil,
    green shoots rose up from the soil,
the cucumber, bean and potato did grow
    accompanying the love apple…the tomato.

During the Great Depression gardens were a necessity
    due to food scarcity,
but the variety helped make a meal complete
    substituting for lack of meat.

One substitute Mom Castner commonly made,
    which Lew found irksome,
was of green tomatoes she would raid
    to slice into stirred eggs and cracker crumb.

Though tomatoes had no chance to ripen
    before Mom again raided the garden,
the frying and serving of each coated slice
    provided sustenance for continuing life.

TR

January 31, 2009

Guess My Age

In the spring of 1998 I was a technician
    working in a materials science laboratory,
it was early afternoon when from the model shop
    across the hall entered a worker named Henry.

Henry and I chatted about how people grow older
    and guessing one's age became a subject.
Good food, rest, health, attitude effect appearance
    and to have Henry guess my age I did interject.

Studying me momentarily Henry apprised,
    then said that he thought I was thirty eight.
Actually being forty three I was pleasantly surprised,
    told Henry his guess I did appreciate.

Henry then asked me to guess his age.
    "Forty eight," I replied confidently.
Henry gasped, "Forty eight? I'm not forty eight.
    I'm the same age as you. I'm forty three."

I noticed that Henry's point was quite emphatic,
    he departed shortly after I was apologetic.
He guessed I was five years younger and I guessed
    he was five years older…how ironic.

My coworker David came in and enthusiastically
    I told him about Henry and what had transpired.
I urged David that he could be an objective observer,
    planning for Henry's return we conspired.

Late that afternoon Henry reentered the lab,
    conversationally I sought to reengage,
returning to the earlier subject I suggested that
    maybe David, being objective, could guess our age?

Henry was agreeable so I called out 'nonchalantly',
    "David." He didn't seem to hear me initially,
"ummm…David." He looked over at me…and Henry,
    of the subject I gave a brief summary.

I implored David that Henry and I were asking him
    as an objective observer for our ages to estimate.
He agreed and I asked him to guess mine first,
    David said, "Thirty eight."

"Wow…thirty eight, that's the same age that Henry
    had guessed. I feel good," I said happily.
"How old do you think Henry is?" I asked.
    David said, "Fifty three."

Henry cried out loudly, "What?! Fifty three?!
    I'm not fifty three!"
I figured that David would say forty eight instead
    of fifty three, which surprised even me.

Henry looked at us…then uttered, "Ohhhh,
    …you guys got me good!"
We all laughed and I was quite satisfied this went
    just the way I thought it should.

TR

Habitual Suer – Jim Rue.

February 23, 1981

Habitual Suer

Jim went shopping at Hillcrest, circa 1971,
    to seek a product in which to invest.
A woman shopper he could see
    was looking about quite suspiciously.

Suddenly she appeared to fall
    upon the floor in the mall.
The woman moaned that she did ache,
    the store manager's arrival did not long take.

She said that she fell on the slippery floor,
    her body felt quite sore.
Upon the store she was placing the blame,
    saying she might file a medical claim.

The manager helped the woman to her feet,
    asking of the fall did anyone see?
The woman hopefully pointed to Jim nearby,
    and as a witness Jim did agree.

Jim said that while making a purchase
    he saw the woman fall on purpose,
and that any claim she might make
    would be that of a fake.

Jim's words left the woman speechless,
    apparently she had heard enough.
The woman regathered her belongings
    and departed in a huff.

The manager thanked Jim for his statement
    which could contest the claimant,
of the woman the manager knew her,
    she's reputed to be a habitual suer.

TR

85

December 23, 2006

Half-Drowned

At West Virginia Wesleyan I took Lifesaving Class
    my first year, during the fall semester.
On November 7, 1972, I was tested and passed all,
    but for rescuing the victim in the water.

The instructor flunked me on the basis
    that I lacked confidence,
and was afraid of the water…I was disappointed,
    but the decision made sense.

I repeated Lifesaving during the spring semester,
    Lee, a lifeguard who assisted the instructor,
taunted me that he was going to play my water victim,
    and would struggle against me strongly…for sure.

Lee was shorter than me by a couple of inches,
    but his body was quite stocky,
being much stronger than me and with his determination,
    to successfully rescue him would be rocky.

The night of April 9, 1973 was my Lifesaving test,
    and when it became time for the water victim part
Lee was in the water at the other end of the Olympic-size
    pool…waiting for me…it was time to start.

I dove in on the shallow end of the pool,
    swam down towards the deeper end slowly
so that I wouldn't be tired by the time I reached him,
    then stopped a short distance from Lee.

Lee was facing me and the pool's shallow end, splashing,
    I came in close to grab his lower right arm,
to roll him into a cross-chest tow…at me he lunged
    …I backed away in alarm.

Lee splashed some...daring me to try another approach,
     I pushed myself beneath the surface,
swam underneath him and came up from behind,
     quickly put my left arm across his chest in place.

I moved my left hip into Lee's back...rolled onto my side,
     and began using the side stroke, ready to brace
for the coming...whirlwind...splashing...thrashing...
     I struggled to keep him and myself above the surface.

We struggled...he broke loose from my grip...turned,
     up out of the water...at me Lee lunged,
wrapped his arms around me in a front head hold,
     beneath the surface we plunged.

We sank underneath...I tucked my chin down,
     grabbed Lee's hips with my hands...pushed upward
and turned him around...moved into the cross-chest tow,
     started swimming the side stroke moving forward.

Lee began tossing and turning, thrashing about,
     we dipped under the water intermittently,
I tried to maintain my grip and keep our heads up
     ...I then held him under purposely.

 With his stamina greater than mine, using up my energy,
     I determined that if I had to struggle with Lee
it was just as easy to hold him underneath me,
     ...he thrashed about vainly.

When his struggling ceased I rolled him up and over,
     and allowed him to breathe...I continued swimming.
We went a short distance and Lee resumed thrashing,
     I rolled him under until he stopped struggling.

Eventually Lee stopped...no more thrashing around,
     I pivoted him to the surface...half-drowned?
He played a passive victim, which did not forestall
     my being able to cross-chest tow him to the pool wall.

Upon the deck, I placed his forearms as he slouched,
    I climbed out, turned, held his wrists and crouched,
pulled Lee up in a vertical lift, then lowered him to the deck,
    then it was time to do a respiratory check.

Lee did me a favor testing my limits in Lifesaving Class
    and by the end of that evening I did pass.
I became a lifeguard at Wesleyan my junior year.
    It is wise to approach the water with respect and fear.

TR

Handcuffed

I arrived back at West Virginia Wesleyan College
    on December 2, 1974, after Thanksgiving vacation.
Bill, my roommate and his girlfriend had returned earlier,
    he worried for me; I survived a head-on collision.

Bill put his handcuffs on himself and his girlfriend,
    but then could not find the key.
It was a blessing that they had their clothes on
    or there'd be embarrassment due to immodesty.

Bill's spontaneous joke was lost on his girlfriend,
    who was chagrined about the situation.
We decided to find a policeman with a master key,
    probably at the local police station.

It was dark out; we drove down to the police station,
    located in the center of Buckhannon.
We ascended the steps and the door was open,
    we entered…the lights were on.

No policeman was manning the front desk,
    nor was there any within sight.
We called out, walked around, checked in rooms,
    the station was deserted on site?

'The lights were on but no one was home'
    could be taken literally.
Did they leave in a hurry…on an emergency?
    Maybe they went for coffee?

One of us remembered a small restaurant
    on a nearby side street.
We decided to take a chance and walked over, entered,
    hoping of a policeman we would meet.

In a side booth were uniformed policemen three,
    eating doughnuts and drinking coffee.
The three of us approached them gingerly,
    they looked up at us curiously.

What was happening, one cop did demand,
    Bill explained and raised his handcuffed hand
showing how he and his girlfriend were shackled,
    and the three policemen chuckled.

One of the policemen rose up from his seat,
    released Bill and his girlfriend with a key,
but he confiscated the handcuffs with no argument
    from us...we departed hastily and happily.

The lesson I learned from this experience,
    especially in regards to my wife Mary,
is that before we ever use our handcuffs...first...
    we always make sure we have the key.

TR

July 4, 2007

Here Comes the Bride

Our auburn haired, 20-year-old daughter Cathy
    was asked by her friend Arnaldo
to attend a wedding for one of his college buddies,
    she excitedly planned to go.

Arnaldo attended Ramapo College for undergraduate study,
    became friends with an African-American lady,
and was invited to her December 23, 2006 wedding,
    to be held at a resort in northeastern New Jersey.

Cathy drove her maroon-colored Cutlass Ciera
    from Pennsylvania to Paterson, New Jersey,
on the afternoon of the wedding day, down Route 80,
    to meet with Arnaldo and greet his family.

Before getting dressed for the wedding,
    Arnaldo needed to make a final stop
to get a haircut, so Cathy drove him
    to the D'Classe Beauty Parlor & Barber Shop.

Cathy and Arnaldo returned, and he dressed
    in a black suit and a tie colored maroon,
his shirt was purple and matched her jewelry,
    then off to the wedding they'd depart soon.

Cathy was draped in a brown and cream colored dress,
    an accompanying black sweater was worn,
black, high heel shoes encased her feet,
    her neck…a purple necklace did adorn.

Departing before six thirty, it was rainy,
    and increased traffic made them late,
the wedding was to start at seven thirty
    but they arrived at eight.

Here Comes the Bride – Cathy Rue.

Once parked…they ran…her in high heels,
    in a new, brown, corduroy coat Cathy was cloaked,
accidentally…into a deep puddle she poked,
    her right foot emerged soaked.

Arnaldo and Cathy rushed into the resort,
    hurried along the first floor corridor,
at the end they entered the elevator,
    and ascended up to the second floor.

The elevator doors slid open…and to the right
    stood the bride and her father,
in front were bridesmaids, and to the left,
    at the chapel's doors awaited an usher.

Arnaldo gave the bride a hug in greeting.
    "I will wait a few minutes," the bride did tell,
"so you can get in there first," she did compel.
    Arnaldo and Cathy approached the chapel.

As the usher opened the angled doors wide
    music began playing 'Here Comes the Bride',
everyone turned to see the bridal party in sight…
    instead witnessed the only woman who's white.

Arnaldo and Cathy walked straight ahead
    to sit in the opposite last pew,
in front of the sound 'dude' playing the music,
    now they'd have a complete view.

The bridesmaids followed as the ceremony did progress,
    entered the pretty black bride in her pretty white dress,
subsequently, eight more people showed up tardy,
    but were on time for the reception party.

Arnaldo and Cathy were positioned at the reception,
    along with an African-American couple,
they were seated to the left and at the farthest location
    from the bride and groom's head table.

Everyone was friendly, and Cathy enjoyed herself,
    moving from table to table went the bride and groom,
Arnaldo introduced Cathy to the newly married couple,
    dancing and socializing permeated the room.

When Arnaldo and Cathy departed the reception,
    in traffic they became lost twice,
Cathy needed to turn left…not in the right direction,
    despite inconvenience…the occasion was nice.

TR

May 2, 1981

Hospital Design

In the spring of 1980
    Gram did not feel well.
An appointment was made with her doctor
    due to her ailing spell.

The doctor couldn't confirm a diagnosis,
    an appointment at the hospital was made.
In order to make a medical hypothesis
    the doctor wanted Gram to be X-rayed.

Gram was ushered to an inner room
    at the local hospital.
She was told to disrobe for the X-rays
    that are internally visual.

Gram was given a loose hospital gown,
    she donned it with a frown
because by being elderly she had poor circulation,
    the hospital had air-cooled ventilation.

Gram had to await the technician's arrival,
    as time elapsed she shivered.
shaking in her seat…from the cold
    she wished to be delivered.

Eventually the technician did arrive,
    of doctor's orders he'd fulfill,
the technician took the X-rays of Gram,
    and Gram had taken to chill.

Gram came back home with a cold
    caused by the hospital design
and with the ventilation system chilling patients
    it proves to be asinine.

TR

Icicles – Rue Home at Camp Pahaquarra, about 1961.

December 15, 1981

Icicles

Early childhood was spent at Camp Pahaquarra,
    an established Boy Scout camp.
We were year round residents in summer dry
    and in winter damp.

The approach of winter brought the cold
    with a cover of snow,
and along the eaves forming in a row
    icicles began to grow.

Over the eaves water droplets would trickle,
    dribbling until the cold could capture,
adding to the formation of each icicle,
    creating an array of frozen sculpture.

Icicles hung in muted silence...
    but in the sun they'd glisten.
Formation of multipointed clumps occurred
    with the roof fully laden.

Occasionally an icicle reaching as a stalactite
    joined to the base of a stalagmite,
forming from roof to ground a column
    like an ancient pillar standing solemn.

Warmth of spring sun resulted in icicle dripping,
    burrowing through snow to rotting leaves,
the seasonal enemy weakened frozen gripping
    causing crashing down from the eaves.

Broken into chunks of frozen debris,
    lay the icicle array,
being part of nature's scheme I could see
    as they melted away.

TR

December 25, 2007

Instant Messaging

It was in the early spring of the year 2005,
    I sat at the table on that cold, dark evening,
my daughter Beth Ann was typing on the computer
    with her friend Jonna…instant messaging.

Only Bangor High seniors and juniors could ask
    somebody else to accompany them to the prom,
Beth Ann began laughing along with typing…I wondered
    about the commotion interrupting the calm.

Cathy as a senior and Beth Ann as a junior could go
    but 15-year-old Dan was only a freshman.
Jonna was being pressured to take him by Beth Ann,
    but she was impersonating her brother Dan.

Into the living room came Dan, Cathy and Mary,
    they stood behind Beth Ann in order to see
and all laughed over the incident
    while Beth Ann pursued Dan's 'intent'.

Jonna explained to 'Dan' that she expected
    to be asked to the prom by a certain fellow,
the young man was an upperclassman
    and with him she intended to go.

'Dan' would not take "No" for an answer,
    he really wanted to go Beth Ann insisted,
and ignored any excuse Jonna had to offer,
    as her brother Beth Ann persisted.

Jonna was becoming more insistent
    that she would not be Dan's date.
Beth Ann, Dan, Cathy and Mary enjoyed the merriment
    but Jonna was becoming irate.

"Ha…ha…ha…this is really Beth Ann,"
 she ended stringing her friend along.
Jonna typed in her response, "Ha…ha…ha
 …I knew it all along."

Subsequently, Jonna's intended escort retracted
 his invitation right before the prom, it was late,
so she, ironically, asked Dan to accompany her,
 he attended as her prom date.

TR

February 7, 1981

Irene Castle's Bob...Fobbed

Len courted Mae in spring 1919,
    being attracted to features fair.
He found her blue eyes alluring
    and especially her long, brunette hair.

Early on in marriage Len liked to braid
    Mae's hair streaked brown...not blonde.
Of the feel of the hair in his hands
    he was quite fond.

In 1926 Len accompanied Mae's brothers
    to Canada for a vacation,
whereupon Mae decided to have her hair cut
    after serious consideration.

Irene Castle had introduced a new hairstyle
    that immediately became popular.
She bobbed her hair providing convenience,
    others imitated the dance star.

Disappointment...Len felt when he returned,
    saw Mae's hair bobbed.
When they retired later that evening
    Len still felt fobbed.

Propped up on an elbow Len lamented,
    "Why did you do it?
I never wanted you to have it cut,"
    being verbally explicit.

Neither could sleep throughout the night,
    Mae's action made Len fret.
Being the rare occasion when Len could be provoked
    caused Mae to be upset

Irene Castle's Bob…Fobbed – Leonard and Mae Sellner Rue.

The following morning Len addressed Mae's Ma,
    "She doesn't look like my Mary."
Time softened the discontent that Len felt
    Mae's impulsive action was contrary.

Eventually Mae grew back its length,
    in time gray streaked the hair,
for the remainder of their lives together
    Len braided with loving care.

TR

February 12, 1981

Japanese Grenadier

In spring of 1945 Al was in the U.S. Army's
    24th Corps, 7th Division and the 32nd Regiment.
Objective was to capture South Pacific islands from the Japs,
    Okinawa became Al's command's encampment.

During the day the army would push inland,
    confronting Japanese willing to make a stand.
During the night the army would dig in and hold position
    and keep watchful eyes for attack from the opposition.

Prior to nightfall square perimeters termed 'foxholes'
    were dug a foot deep into the rocky coral,
a parapet of stone and dirt built up the foxhole's peripheral
    and one contained Al, a sleepy private and a corporal.

Nightly, Al and his companions strung out trip grenades,
    the rings were attached to elevated wire, fastened to a stake.
If a Jap approached and jarred the wire line,
    an explosion a loose grenade would make.

One night Al was on the right wing front line,
    his foxhole was second from the end.
No one left the foxholes at night,
    and it made them easier to defend.

Usually, the private that was always sleepy
    was the one given the first night duty,
but for the 10:00 two-hour watch Al volunteered,
    agreement came from companions once conferred.

Al scanned with eyes around the perimeter,
    peering from beneath his helmet.
With gun resting against the parapet,
    all was still…and quiet.

Japanese Grenadier – Al Mease, 1945.

Al saw the clouds high up
    quickly passing by the face of the half moon,
his comrades slept soundly next to him
    on this night in early June.

At midnight Al made a last 360 degree inspection,
    there was no sign of any Japanese.
He turned to wake up Sleepy to relieve him
    so that he could catch some Zs.

A movement behind caught his eye,
    Al grabbed up a gun.
Al realized it wasn't his, retrieved his own
    and quickly aimed his M-1.

Al pushed off the safety with his finger,
    an up and down movement he did see.
Aiming low Al squeezed the trigger
    firing one…two…three.

Neither shape nor movement could Al discern,
    the disappearance of his target raised concern.
Out in front a grenade did explode,
    for a Jap the trip line bore ill bode.

Al and the men in the last foxhole
    fired simultaneously, all were tense.
Four shots Al fired forward,
    then along the front there was silence.

Streaking high through the dark sky,
    turning night into day burst flares.
Al and his aroused comrades faced the front,
    a dead Jap was seen with their stares.

A call of inquiry came down the line,
    response returned that all were fine.
The sleepy private went back to nap.
    Al wondered about the first Jap.

Could the Jap be the same as the one up front,
    or between the foxholes where Al saw a crater?
Or could he be hiding behind a dense bush in back,
    to check he'd have to wait until later.

Al and the corporal remained on guard,
    with neither sleepy throughout the night.
Al maintained a close scrutiny
    keeping the crater and the bush in sight.

At first light at the crack of dawn,
    to the crater Al's curiosity was drawn.
Over the foxhole Al crawled out,
    "Get back in!" the captain did shout.

Night coolness faded with the rising sun,
    soldiers basked in the area quite sunny.
Al was anxious to inspect the area,
    He moved to the crater with cautious scrutiny.

Slumped down in the crater were a corpse and a grenade.
    The up and down movement Al had detected
was the tapping of a pin into a grenade top,
    Al's action prevented the grenade being activated.

A self-applied bandage hung around the leg,
    a bullet had shattered the right kneecap.
A bullet had pierced above the heart,
    bleeding sapped life from the Jap.

Al glanced at the medical insignia on the collar,
    the Jap medic had become a grenadier.
Al felt regret at taking a life,
    but recognized the duty as a soldier.

TR

106

December 20, 2006

Jesus Wept

"Jesus wept."
    God in flesh was born into his humanity,
thus Jesus Christ experienced His creation,
    of the physical and emotional attributes, in humility.

Jesus was tired in Samaria, in John 4:6,
    "Now Jacob's well was there." Scripture did tell,
"Jesus therefore, being wearied with his journey,
    sat thus on the well:"

From Jerusalem, to Bethany, Jesus and disciples did go,
    in Mark 11:12, "And on the morrow
when they were come from Bethany,
    he was hungry:"

In John 1:46, Philip sought to introduce Jesus,
    "And Nathanael said unto him," perhaps amusedly,
"Can there any good thing come out of Nazareth?
    Philip saith unto him, Come and see."

Praise was offered in John 1:47, "Jesus saw Nathanael
    coming to him," stating, perhaps with a smile,
"Behold an Israelite indeed,
    in whom is no guile!"

"And Jesus went into the temple of God," in Matthew 21:12,
    viewed 'the den of thieves' that righteously angers,
"and cast out all them that sold and bought in the temple,
    and overthrew the tables of the moneychangers,"

His love reached out to all in Matthew 19:14,
    "But Jesus said, Suffer little children
and forbid them not, to come onto me:
    for of such is the kingdom of heaven."

After Lazarus, his friend had died; Jesus came to the tomb.
    In John 11:32, Lazarus' sister, named Mary did confide
to Jesus when "she fell down at his feet, saying unto him,
    Lord, if thou hadst been here, my brother had not died."

"When Jesus therefore saw her weeping, and the Jews
    also weeping which came with her," being Mary,
"he groaned in the spirit, and was troubled."
    described in John 11:33.

Jesus was going to raise Lazarus from the dead,
    though his friend had died four days earlier, and yet
in John 11:35, the anguish of the mourners was felt,
    "Jesus wept."

TR

July 1, 1982

<u>July Morn</u>

The sky is light with blue on high,
    along tree tops a gray,
the shadowed greens of lush foliage
    fend for light where they stay.

Birds call distinctive notes with clarity,
    the grass is bedecked with dew,
in our home on Ostrander Road
    I lay before the view.

Lying bare atop covers next to Mary,
    a multicolored quilt does adorn,
she and Critter, our calico cat,
    rest snuggly this July morn.

Feeling the fresh coolness,
    I part curtains before the screened window
and observe to the eastern horizon
    an arising solar glow.

Through the leaves…a sparkle
    heralding the approach of the sun,
it awashes across the landscape,
    day in earnest has begun.

TR

October 29, 1981

<u>Kathy's Concern</u>

I had courted Mary a couple of years
    when one afternoon we had a date,
she wasn't ready upon my arrival,
    to the living room I went to wait.

An overcast darkened the living room
    due to being cloudy,
I settled on the couch sensing gloom,
    was startled to see somebody.

Mary's sister Kathy sat still in a chair,
    she was twelve years of age.
Cancer afflicted the maturing girl's personage
    and she demonstrated much courage.

Chemotherapy and radiation altered Kathy's physique
    causing features to become gaunt,
but her strength of spirit
    the disease did not daunt.

Kathy raised her head in deep thought,
    my attention she then sought,
"Mary's special…she's a good sister.
    You take good care of her."

Kathy expressed herself in a way
    that I thought urgent,
we exchanged a look across the room…silent
    for a searching moment.

Kathy questioned, "Do you hear me…"
    for my answer she prodded,
"…take good care of her…"
    my head I nodded.

Kathy's Concern – Kathleen Alice Jago.

Of my response Kathy did discern,
    stared forward from her chair,
and I pondered over Kathy's concern
    for Mary's future care.

I wasn't sure then of what to say,
    looked out at the day cast gray.
I realized impossibility while gazing at the pane
    for me to feel her inner pain.

Mary entered with warmth of a sunray,
    being ready to go our way,
I noticed while taking our departure
    Kathy painting a stoic picture.

Cancer won its battle with Kathy in April 1978,
    a year and a half it harried,
but her love for her older sister lives on
    and Mary and I married.

TR

March 8, 1981

Kiboko's Use

In 1970 Len bought a kiboko while visiting Zambia,
     a whip made out of hippopotamus hide.
Later, Len and his guide wished to return from Rhodesia,
     stopping for a border check they had to abide.

A Negroid border guard approached their vehicle,
     posed questions such as the purchase of any souvenir.
Len replied that their purchases were covered due to dust,
     the guard felt through the blanket over the gear.

Feeling the whip…the guard gave a questioning glance,
     and wanted it identified as part of his inquiry.
"A kiboko," Len replied…changing the guard's countenance.
     The guard had suddenly become angry.

Whites used to lash blacks using the kiboko with abuse,
     the black guard was upset about its intended use.
Seeking a hasty way to end the strife,
     Len said, "It's for the wife."

The guard's lips grinned…then beamed with a smile
     nodding with comprehension.
The guard waved Len and the guide across the border
     without undue hesitation.

TR

June 14, 2009

La Vie en Rose

"Hold me close and hold me fast
    The magic spell you cast
This is La Vie en Rose," Edith Piaf did croon
    an English version of this French tune.

"When you kiss me heaven sighs
    And though I close my eyes
I see La Vie en Rose," Edith did continue,
    I listened on a YouTube venue.

"When you press me to your heart
    I'm in a world apart
A world where roses bloom," Edith beckoned,
    music and lyrics moved me I reckoned.

A 1930s Parisian street performer Edith Piaf's
    popularity internationally arose
singing torch songs with a mezzo-soprano voice,
    her signature song was La Vie en Rose.

"La Vie en Rose" translates to "Life is Pink",
    meaning life is beautiful.
Edith's accented rendition elicited emotion
    registering a future quite hopeful.

"Give your heart and soul to me
    And life will always be
La Vie en Rose," Edith paused at this…
    ending the song with an audible kiss.

This song pulled forward in time a memory
    from cold January 1977
when I wooed an Irish rose named Mary,
    snow covered the landscape then.

Mary and I sought shelter from the cold
    inside my Mom's Paul Street abode,
we spread blankets and pillows on the rug
    to lie together comfortably snug.

The television glare provided the only light
    glowing in the dark of night,
Saturday Night Live began playing on the screen
    and together we did closely lean.

In the subdued light together Mary and I pressed,
    our lips tentatively caressed,
hesitancy receded…our smooching compressed
    and mutual affection was expressed.

Interplay with tongues added to the caresses,
    intensity overwhelmed the senses,
unplanned…our locked lips bussed continuous
    making this kiss quite sensuous.

Time began to slow…slow…slowing was conveyed
    while surroundings seemed to fade,
our existence entered a state that was surreal,
    only the lingering kiss remained real.

Saturday Night Live was off the air
    when our lips did part,
an hour and a half had passed away unnoticed
    which gave me a start.

Reality seeped back into our earthly realm
    from a state that did overwhelm,
regaining our bearings we sought to compose
    from a state of 'La Vie en Rose'.

We folded the blankets and replaced the pillows,
    I returned Mary home to the Jagos,
the song 'La Vie en Rose' allowed us to reminisce
    over a most memorable kiss.

TR

August 5, 2006

<u>Launched Like a Rocket</u>

Len, my older brother headed home from work
    and at 6 P.M. on October 2, 2002 it was sunny
as he sped southward on the four-lane Route 33
    straddling a Hog…his Harley.

Len purchased his motorcycle in 1996,
    it was a Harley Dyna Superglide
and weighed greater than 600 pounds,
    at 7000 miles it was an occasional ride.

Len wore hiking boots on his feet,
    a helmet on his head provided protection,
he steered his Harley in the right lane
    approaching the Beaver Valley Road intersection.

A couple of cars were in front of Len,
    their right turn signals began blinking,
they began to slow down to turn onto Beaver Valley
    where a lady driving a hatchback was waiting.

The hatchback on Beaver Valley Road was northbound,
    its left light blinking was observed,
and Len figured he would zip around them all,
    into the passing lane he swerved.

The hatchback now blocked his passing lane waiting
    to head northward…Len's eyes grew wide!
Southward was where the woman driver was looking,
    he was going to hit her broadside!

In front of the hatchback's rear tire the Harley collided,
    pushed the car's rear back about 7 feet and yet
even as Len's left foot also hit he confided,
    "I was launched like a rocket."

116

Over the hatchback Len sailed through the air
    20 to 25 feet beyond the accident,
he tucked his head down…dropped…
    tumbled 15 feet further on the pavement.

Len rolled to rest in the passing lane,
    raised his head where he had lain,
the hatchback's woman driver he could see
    and she was crying hysterically.

While Len lay in the middle of the road
    from the northbound lanes across the median
came Wilma, a high school nurse he knows
    offering help as a Good Samaritan.

Len rose up from his prostrate position
    and with Wilma providing assistance
he was able to walk off the road,
    and awaited the arrival of an ambulance.

To call home Wilma let Len use her phone,
    he first asked what's for dinner of his wife Joan,
she answered his routine question and then he did state,
    "We will be eating a little late."

At Pocono Hospital Len's boot was removed,
    his left foot was black and blue,
three hours later while lying on a gurney
    his left ankle began to hurt too.

Len's left ankle was found to be sprained,
    for three weeks crutches provided support,
the job is never finished until the paperwork is done
    so he waited for the insurance report.

The woman driver's insurance company paid Len
    since the Harley was totaled in the accident
and he was able to buy Joan a car
    as a consequence of this event.

TR

September 4, 1981

Leg Crimp

In 1970 Jim walked home from school
    along shaded Oxford Street.
He saw three kids waiting ahead where
    Oxford and Prospect meet.

Jim recognized Reggie, a bully built skinny
    waiting at the corner sunny.
Of Jim's path Reggie and friends did intercept,
    where they intentionally kept.

The bully made a threatening advance towards Jim
    prompting a tussle.
Both fell to the ground
    and the two began to wrestle.

Jim caught Reggie's head in a maneuver
    between his legs…above the knees.
Jim interlocked his ankles making a lever,
    upon Reggie's neck he did squeeze.

Jim maintained a strong pressure
    creating the leg crimp.
Reggie became a helpless, struggling figure
    who suddenly went limp.

Releasing the bully slumped motionless
    to stand up rose Jim,
observing the prostrate form lying lifeless
    he thought, "I've killed him."

A circle of kids had formed around them,
    his gym bag Jim did retrieve.
Jim walked through the group to head home,
    from the scene he took his leave.

With concern about killing the skinny creep
    Jim pondered his fate.
Witnesses would know where to direct the police,
    at home he'd wait.

To the door came a witnessing lad
    who informed that Reggie did revive.
This information made Jim feel glad
    that his antagonist was still alive.

Jim's leg crimp had blocked blood to the brain
    preventing passage of oxygen
resulting in the bully's consciousness to drain,
    Reggie never bothered Jim again.

TR

January 26, 2006

Little Divil

Great Aunt Mary Claire Kempsey DeRose was an older sister
    to Mary's grandmother, Margaret Rose Kempsey Jago,
and after her husband, Frank died in 1964 she was a widow
    living on South Side, Easton, in a homey bungalow.

Great Aunt Mary was known as 'Aunt May' affectionately,
    physically, her upper body was built stocky,
supported atop 'two chicken legs' as described by Mary,
    and Aunt May had a no-nonsense personality.

Mary and her older brothers and sisters
    took turns going to visit at Aunt May's.
this tale occurred in 1968 when 12-year old Linda
    accompanied 9-year old Mary there for a few days.

Near Aunt May's home on Charles Street
    was a small, South Side neighborhood bakery,
it was a treat to visit and for a dime
    you could buy an eight-inch diameter cookie.

Aunt May attended St Bernard's Church, founded in 1829,
    the oldest Roman Catholic Church in the Lehigh Valley,
in 1836 the church was dedicated at 132 South 5th Street,
    along with an adjoining Gallows Hill cemetery.

Gallows Hill was a name given to the scene of execution,
    for three soldiers, after each received a murder conviction,
of a Stroudsburg tavern keeper, prior to Sullivan's expedition,
    in 1779, during the American Revolution.

This particular Sunday, Aunt May did not go to church,
    and she gave two dimes to the two girls each,
intending for them to put the coins into the collection plate,
    to the chapel they'd have to walk in order to reach.

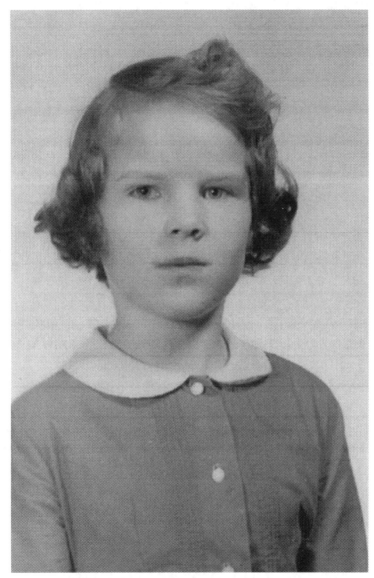

Little Divil – Mary Margaret Jago.

Together Mary and Linda departed from Charles Street,
    descended from Lachenour to North Smith Avenue,
down steep, stone steps, holding onto a black railing,
    with an elevated railroad trestle in view.

Mary's family attended St. Philip and James normally,
    located across the river, in Phillipsburg, New Jersey
where her Dad would lead them up front to sit for mass,
    and two separate collections would make a pass.

At St Bernard's when the collection plate went around
    Mary put in just the one dime,
and expected another collection before the service ended,
    but it was not taken a second time.

Mary clutched the remaining dime tightly and yet
    the misunderstanding made the young girl fret,
otherwise she'd have gladly put it in the collection plate,
    but was now afraid Aunt May would be upset.

Returning after the morning mass at St. Bernard,
    Mary and Linda climbed up the steep steps then,
having to face Great Aunt May would be hard,
    and Mary suffered…feeling guilt ridden.

With fear of displeasing God, the church and Aunt May,
    Mary's knees trembled as she uttered, with trepidation,
"There was only one offering at the tavern.
    I put in one dime. What do I do with the other one?"

"You little divil!" Aunt May replied indignantly.
    "It's a chapel, not a tavern!
You kept that dime to spend it at the bakery,"
    she accused Mary, being quite stern.

Being accused of a falsehood upset Mary,
    but she retained the dime…so off to the bakery,
she purchased a large chocolate chip cookie,
    shared it with Linda…relished the treat with glee.

TR

122

September 22, 1981

Loading Hay

Harold hated farm work
    but Betty's Pop had a broken baler,
needed help on loading hay
    being a manual chore.

Harold came with Betty and the kids
    after completing his work shift.
He planned to assist in loading the hay,
    into the truck he'd lift.

Pop had given his young farmhand Jimmy
    the whole day off,
and with the job needing to be done,
    it caused Harold to scoff.

But up to the field went three
    Pop, Betty and Harold.
Betty was picked to drive the truck,
    Pop and Harold would load.

Betty drove slowly across the field,
    the men followed in stride.
Pop was on the upper side throwing down,
    Harold threw from the lower side.

Jimmy came to help on the second load,
    joined Pop in throwing down.
Harold labored tossing up into the truck,
    doing it made him frown.

After working all day Harold was tired,
    to throw down he then preferred.
He verbalized his suggestion to exchange sides,
    Pop and Jimmy reluctantly transferred.

The truck was piled high with hay,
    the loading done…whew.
Harold climbed into the truck to drive,
    Pop came up to argue.

To drive to the barn Harold had planned,
    to drive himself Pop did demand
claiming that if he didn't one could expect
    that enroute the hay would upset.

Harold climbed out at his father-in-law's insistence
    due to being balked.
Harold took Betty's hand in his,
    down the lane they walked.

Harold and Betty looked back up the hill,
    onto the road appeared the truck.
Suddenly half the load of hay did spill.
    My…what rotten luck.

Harold said to Betty, "Let's get the kids,"
    disregarding where hay now lain,
"…and head home," Harold stated,
    and they proceeded on down the lane.

TR

July 23, 1981

Loose Lugnuts

In 1940 Dot had in her possession
    a black Model A Ford,
the car was given by her father,
    each side graced with a running board.

The Model A received maintenance work
    at Cookie's garage in Belvidere,
upon completion one sunny day
    homeward Dot did steer.

Near the Schneiber homestead,
    something moving registered surprise,
a wheel rolled passed the driver's side,
    Dot viewed with widened eyes.

When Dot realized it was her wheel
    the moment…tense.
The rolling wheel ran off the road,
    jumped a farmer's fence.

Over the fence the wheel hopped,
    into the field it flopped.
Dot braked the car…it stopped,
    the left corner rear dropped.

The car settled…the wheel lay flat,
    off the running board Dot stepped down.
To seek aid and an explanation
    she began walking back to town.

A worker at Cookie's was embarrassed
    due to evidence of negligence
of loose lugnuts not having been tightened
    and a wheel over the fence.

TR

December 19, 2006

<u>Losing a Friend</u>

Proverbs 17:17 states, "A friend loveth at all times,
    and a brother is born for adversity."
The conflict of contentious brothers is told,
    as part of the Bible story.

These contentious brothers included: Cain and Abel,
    Isaac and Ishmael, Jacob and Esau,
Adonijah and Solomon, and Joseph's brothers who sold
    him into slavery…their treachery left a pall.

I have two brothers: Len, who is five years older,
    and Jim, who is two years younger.
Over the years we have fought and played together
    a lot…as expected with someone having a brother.

In 7th grade, at school in Blairstown, in the fall of 1966,
    I met Ray, a kid my size, who liked the outdoors, trapping,
my naturalist father, and for us a friendship was made,
    so to each other's home we went visiting.

Ray rode home with me on our school bus, in the fall of 1967,
    to stay with my family for the weekend,
his folks were to pick him up on Sunday afternoon,
    until then I had a good time with Jim and my friend.

We waited, in the middle of that Sunday afternoon,
    for Ray's parents to come pick him up soon.
Jim, Ray and I began tossing around a basketball for fun,
    in the front yard near the porch, under the autumn sun.

After a short time, whenever Ray would get the ball,
    instead of playing a nice game of catch,
he aimed, threw it hard trying to hit Jim in the legs or body,
    if it bounced away Jim ended up having to play fetch.

This obnoxious behavior on Ray's part continued unabated,
    I did not understand why Jim did not complain.
Then I figured that because Ray was my friend and guest
    that was why of complaining Jim did refrain.

I held onto the basketball when next it came to me,
    told Ray that this game of catch was to be friendly,
he ignored me completely, continued hitting Jim repeatedly,
    my temper flared up, I got the ball, acted quickly.

I aimed and threw the basketball hard into his face,
    the blow stunned Ray as he stood in place.
I quickly grabbed up the ball to hold it as a weapon,
    Ray sputtered, "What's going on?"

We were supposed to be playing a nice game of tossing
    the basketball around…to Ray, I did expound,
but he continued to try to hit my brother even after
    I had warned him to stop messing around.

I could see anger cloud his face…flash in his eyes,
    now I had to fight…I did realize.
Dropping the ball…I charged forward…lunged
    …grabbed Ray…thrust forward…to the ground we plunged!

I landed on top of Ray when we hit the ground,
    I quickly moved to sit astride his middle,
grabbed his wrists to pin them back and down,
    held on tight as he bucked in struggle.

Beneath me Ray used his strength and wiggled,
    in his attempt to free himself he struggled,
and I desperately knew I had to hold him tight
    or we would have an extended fight.

Eventually, Ray struggled less and addressed me verbally,
    demanding that I get off of him,
I replied, "No," while I continued to hold him securely,
    explained that he was mean to my brother, Jim.

His struggle to dislodge me failed, but he certainly tried,
    I could see now that he was weepy eyed,
I would let him up if he behaved, I did confide,
    I then released him, ready to fight, but he complied.

Ray was upset but not aggressive; I tried talking to him,
    but he did not want to interact with neither Jim nor me.
I felt tense when his parents arrived to pick him up,
    watched his sullen departure with his family.

Following the departure of their car the driveway dust roiled,
    the sunny day was too nice to be spoiled,
then Jim and I had a good-natured wrestling match,
    rolling and laughing on the side yard's grassy patch.

Ray and I never ever spoke to each other again and within
    two years my family moved away, but in the end,
considering his callous approach to my brother, Jim,
    it was worth losing a friend.

TR

January 20, 1982

Mallards' Malcontent

In 1977 on a sunny, Sunday afternoon,
    to accompany my cousins they invited me,
we beached upstream on the Delaware River
    to prepare to water-ski.

A light breeze blew upstream,
    I patiently but anxiously awaited my turn
as each cousin glided into the shallows,
    sinking upon their return.

During my turn Zach decided to steer
    and Mike would be my spotter,
removing my glasses limited eyesight near,
    I waded into the water.

In the shallows I fitted on the skis,
    wore a buoyant waist belt,
with ski points emersed I held the towline,
    tension I abruptly felt.

Pulled up from my crouch I leaned back…too far
    doing an awkward backwards flip,
upon resurfacing I refitted the skis,
    Zach drove the towline around for my grip.

Mike signaled to Zach I was ready,
    Zach revved forward the motor's force
plucking me up onto the water's surface,
    following the boat's upriver course.

With bent legs I skimmed across the surface,
    thought of Jesus of Galilee
and correlated His walk upon the water
    with modern man's ability to water-ski.

Mallards' Malcontent – Mallard Ducks.

Zach steered the boat back downriver,
    I readied with my stance
and swung around in a centrifugal arc,
    cresting waves with my balance.

We traveled beneath the Belvidere-Riverton Bridge,
    with spectators above watching,
and arced around in a returning sweep,
    skied through a middle opening.

Coming off crests against the surface skis slapped,
    up and back we lapped,
under the bridge I followed the boat's churn,
    prepared for another turn.

Zach steered the curve wider
    sweeping me closer to shore,
why?…prompted me to wonder,
    and towards blurred shapes I bore.

I skied in amongst a flock of mallards
    squawking in their fright,
blurred green heads of drakes and brown hens
    erratically took to flight.

Before…behind…mallards did flutter
    quacking their malcontent,
but I also heard Zach and Mike's laughter,
    heartily enjoying the event.

Zach pulled me up towards the beach,
    I glided in with my ride over.
I retrieved my glasses to view the scene
    of mallards resettling upon the river.

TR

April 5, 1981

Meal Fit for a Chief

Scotty, Homer, Clem and I went snowmobiling
　　on a cold, clear afternoon cast sunny,
twenty some miles north of Maniwaki, Quebec, Canada,
　　in 1977, it was late January.

Homer's friends there owned a restaurant/tavern
　　and gas station up along Route 117,
we dressed bulkily but warmly and with face masks,
　　Clem's movie camera recorded the scene.

Scotty with Homer led off on one snowmobile,
　　Clem and I on the other,
I steered while Clem recorded movie footage
　　over my right or left shoulder.

Following the marked trails through fields and woods
　　winding with many a turn,
I held onto Clem's camera when he steered,
　　later that afternoon we did return.

To make a snowmobile trek up from Maniwaki
　　on the morrow Scotty spoke with speculation.
We loaded up the snowmobiles onto the trailer,
　　headed south to the Kitigan Zibi Indian Reservation.

To check on the snowmobile pin Scotty voiced to pull over,
　　Homer protested late…to the right we did veer,
…suddenly we sank into a deep drainage ditch,
　　settled at about a 45 degree pitch.

Scotty's vehicle was packed in the snow tight,
　　the white stuff had splattered onto the front window,
Homer explained…as we sat there in the semi-light,
　　about deceptive roadside drainage filled with snow.

To exit Scotty's blue Jeep station wagon we climbed up,
    I followed Homer out of the back seat.
The pin holding the snowmobile skies was in place,
    to pull the Jeep and trailer out would be some feat.

We were stuck with no immediate solution,
    Clem and I briefly chuckled over our situation,
but Scotty was concerned with frustration
    about being late for our dinner invitation.

After about 15 to 20 minutes of us being stranded,
    approaching us and heading towards Maniwaki
was a large, logging truck ladened with logs,
    we waved at the driver energetically.

The driver brought his big rig to a stop,
    Scotty engaged him in conversation
only to discover that he did not speak any English,
    but he comprehended our situation.

The driver pulled his truck forward beyond us,
    then backing up a short distance he steered,
a chain was attached from his truck to Scotty's bumper,
    would the bumper break loose Clem wondered?

I asked about whether we should unhook the trailer
    but of our rescue everyone was preoccupied,
the driver, with the chain taut, drove forward pulling both
    Jeep and trailer onto the road…I watched wide-eyed.

Our French Canadian benefactor gathered up his chain,
    Scotty rewarded him with money,
the driver gratefully accepted the gift and then
    drove off in the direction of Maniwaki.

I was surprised that the logging truck had so easily
    pulled both Jeep and trailer out simultaneously
with neither any damage nor even a scratch…lucky,
    we returned to our seats and continued to Maniwaki.

Darkness fell by the time we reached Maniwaki,
    we were tardy for the dinner invitation.
Homer, Scotty, Clem and I rode further onward,
    we arrived at the Kitigan Zibi Reserve in anticipation.

The Reserve of the River Desert or Kitigan Zibi
    Anishinabeg First Nation, an Algonquin band,
lies southwest and is adjacent to the town of Maniwaki
    on 68 square miles of much forested land.

Chief William and his wife Mary invited us to dinner,
    to them Homer has been a long-time friend.
The temperature was below freezing in late January 1977,
    into the warmth of their home we did descend.

William Commanda has worked as a guide, trapper,
    woodsman, craftsman, a birch bark canoe maker,
and was chief of the Algonquin band Kitigan Zibi
    Anishinabeg from 1951 to 1970.

Mary Commanda was a daughter of Charley Smith,
    his Algonquin name was Jan Alawateiwisi.
Charley was a close friend with Homer and for years
    an interpreter for the Hudson Bay Trading Company.

Mary showed us that she was tanning a moose hide
    soaking in a tub in a work area in the basement
while being given a house tour which Clem described,
    "…was very neat and clean, simple but efficient."

Scotty presented the chief with a decanter
    filled with blackberry brandy as a gift.
Mary was prepared to present the food,
    around the table we did shift.

The main course consisted of three dishes:
    beaver, beaver tail and moose nose.
The chief bid us feast with complimentary wishes,
    a portion of moose nose I first chose.

Moose nose was like cow's tongue, tender and tasty,
    as I ate sitting next to the chief.
I reached for beaver as my second delicacy,
    it was like stringy but delicious roast beef.

I lifted to my mouth some beaver tail,
    being oily it was reminiscent of congealed lard.
The chief was involved in verbalizing a tale,
    he then engulfed meat laden with homemade mustard.

I applied the mustard upon some beaver tail,
    engulfing it I felt my mouth become hot!
Taking a quick swig of brandy my throat did sting,
    it was enough 'to gag a maggot'!

We thanked our hostess upon completing the meal
    and into the living room we shifted.
Full of food, warmth made Homer and I peacefully feel
    because into sleep we drifted.

TR

April 5, 1982

Monarchs of Wood

Interspersed in lakes of the north woods
    lie segregated segments of terra firma
that I observed during summers of my youth
    located in eastern Canada.

When the last receding glacier gorged,
    lakes and islands were forged,
whereupon wildlife entered this evolving biome
    filling niches that became home.

Birch and cedar, pine and spruce all white
    compete for space in their life's fight,
withstanding the elements while reaching to the sky,
    living to root…and die.

Each island is a kingdom with water confines
    as observation allowed me to reflect
that the monarchs of wood are the white pines
    to which other species appear subject.

Other species surround centrally located white pines
    with branches slanting in submissive bows.
White pines tower high in protective stances
    stretching outward arms of evergreen boughs.

Towering high above crowns of subjects wooden
    with upturned branches reaching for heaven,
and seeming to approach God with acquiescence
    white pines provide harmony in their essence.

TR

February 7, 1981

Moose Charge

Dad and I were returning from McKinley's railroad depot
    on that August 25, 1977 rainy, overcast day.
A moose was spotted in a clump of spruces,
    Dad pulled the van off the road, out of the way.

Though the weather made for poor photography
    it was the first moose we'd seen so far.
We hoisted on camera equipment,
    with spectators in park bus and car.

Over the embankment we descended,
    through the brush that was wet.
I could discern a bull moose before us
    with large antlers partly covered with velvet.

We positioned ourselves near a lone spruce,
    kept the moose warily in sight.
Dad wondered about the bull being rambunctious, two
    photographers approached back around to our right.

Dad and I ventured forth…about fifty feet
    away from our spruce tree cover.
The moose munched and eyed us nonchalantly,
    the others moved in closer.

"Always keep in your mind
    that if a moose charges," Dad did teach,
"to be prepared to climb a tree
    that you can quickly reach."

I wondered…while looking around
    at the boughs pointing toward the ground,
how could we climb any of these scraggly spruce
    to escape the wrath of an angry moose?

137

Moose Charge – Bull Moose.

Dad was making a camera adjustment…the moose
    charged the others with sudden acceleration,
I nudged Dad on the shoulder and pointed…
    a photographer and the bull ran in our direction!

We dashed back to the lone spruce
    in a rapid pace,
Dad ran behind on one side, I the other,
    gasping for air in the chase.

We crouched low against the trunk,
    the photographer ran in a forward rush.
The moose was only a few feet off
    when the man dove sideways into the brush.

The moose came to halt about 75 feet away
    and threw us each a glance.
He then sauntered back into the brush to our right
    in a triumphant prance.

Dad and I laughed out loud
    at the moose's rambunctious play,
the moose was content with the chase
    and not out for blood today.

TR

More Flowers – Beth Ann Rue.

July 9, 2005

More Flowers

Mary took Cathy, Beth Ann and Dan for a walk
    one June '92' late afternoon,
I settled down to watch TV,
    waiting for their return soon.

Five-year-old Cathy returned holding lavender,
    red carnations and daisies in a bouquet,
gave them to me with instructions
    to arrange in the right way.

Cathy followed me to the kitchen,
    I arranged her flowers in a vase,
and she left when satisfied with
    her bouquet in a proper place.

I sat back down, and then Beth Ann, aged four
    pulled open the door,
"More flowers!"…tossed them on the floor,
    slammed shut the door.

TR

My Wife Mary – Mary Jago Rue.

February 14, 1988

My Wife Mary

My wife's name is Mary,
　　some might think her contrary
but she is kind and caring with nary
　　an imperfection…is my Mary.

Mary had a crush on me
　　when a lassie of thirteen,
I would give her piggyback rides
　　as a lad of seventeen.

Four years later I came a calling,
　　with a rich voice she sung,
played her guitar on sunny afternoons
　　making me feel young.

The sun reflects off reddish brown hair
　　with her features wholesome and fair,
her compassion inspired me to care and pair,
　　and our passion we share.

In daylight or when darkness has fallen
　　over the countryside
her companionship comforts and in bed
　　she's warm by my side.

For our children she's a caring mother,
　　for me a giving lover,
I thank God I was able to marry
　　my wife Mary.

TR

March 12, 2008

Never Again

A blizzard blanketed Rock Springs, Wyoming
    in late April 2005…it kept snowing,
but in the 25 foot long trailer Len and Uschi were 'snug
    as a bug in a rug'.

Naturalist Len Rue the 3ʳᵈ and his wife Uschi
    had headed west from their home in New Jersey
to photograph wildlife, including waterfowl,
    but in Rock Springs the weather turned foul.

Two days later the storm had subsided
    and hearing that more snow was on the way
they decided to go to the Jackson Hole Valley, then
    Yellowstone, started on April 29ᵗʰ, the very next day.

They headed north in a light snow to Jackson Hole,
    near Jackson beautiful spring sunshine gave appeal
for Len and Uschi to photograph various waterfowl
    such as shovelers and Blue-winged Teal.

Len and Uschi settled in for the night at a campground
    with plans to head to Yellowstone then,
however the park road was still closed for the winter,
    but the West Entrance of Yellowstone was open.

They departed the campground the next morning,
    but Uschi clearly saw
that leaving so early was their first mistake
    since nothing had begun to thaw.

Len opted to go over Teton Pass, into Idaho,
    since it was the shorter way to take,
instead of going around by the Snake River Valley,
    to Uschi…this was the second mistake.

Never Again – Uschi and Lennie Rue III.

Wyoming Highway 22 scales the 8,431 foot high pass
    with a maximum 10% grade of the road.
Len and Uschi's Chevrolet Suburban started out
    pulling up their 8,000 pound trailer load.

Raining slightly in the valley…in just three miles
    they ascended 6,000 feet in elevation,
and the weather changed into snow and ice
    which gave cause for consternation.

The highway department had dispersed sparingly
    when they spread out the gravel,
but Len was still grateful it had been done early
    which aided in their treacherous travel.

Topping the summit…ice coated the road,
    it was not a welcome sight.
"Well, that's what prayers, caution and low gears
    are for," Len did cite.

Slowly…Len started down the steep grade,
    through the switchbacks they travelled…slow.
Having visions of sliding…Uschi was afraid
    that they would tumble into the valley below.

When they reached the valley floor finally…safely,
    realizing they had not slipped once even,
Len and Uschi professed thanks to God vocally,
    and both vowed, "Never again!".

TR

January 18, 1981

Nomination

It was 1965 and in sixth grade
    it was time for class officer elections.
Teachers requested nominations
    so that students could make their selections.

I thought of small Kurt for president,
    the office I felt he could justly hold.
You see he was poor, his clothes worn,
    but he had a heart worth of gold.

I raised my hand to declare my choice
    and Kurt was my nomination.
The children broke into laughter
    causing an abrupt termination.

The teachers quieted down the class,
    shortly all the laughter did pass.
The teachers demanded, "What's with the joke?"
    and insisted the nomination I revoke.

Because of Kurt I felt saddened,
    of the anger I felt confused,
with thoughts of right I maddened,
    and of the demand I refused.

In response to my refusal
    I was given an ultimatum,
either remove my nomination
    or visit the principal's sanctum.

I saw all eyes stare at me,
    awaiting my decision.
I felt the confrontation lost,
    recalled Kurt's name as remission.

I did not vote for president.
   I felt it was a mockery.
Manipulations of nominations
   are blows dealt to democracy.

TR

December 21, 2006

<u>Not Another Inch</u>

I came to visit Mary and her family, the Jagos,
    in early 1977, on a wintry Saturday.
Snow covered the landscape along Mountain Lane,
    the weather was good for using a sleigh.

I went sleigh riding with Mary and her family,
    up behind the barn they started a trail, I could see.
The trail went down passed the cherry tree,
    beyond the house, towards the neighbor's property.

Sleigh riding that morning packed the snow tighter,
    which allowed us to go faster and farther.
Someone had made a mound at the end of the run,
    trying to reach it to go airborne was part of the fun.

There were more people than sleds so we teamed up
    in different combinations to sleigh ride,
I rode down with Mary, her siblings or alone, taking turns,
    sitting or stacked on our bellies we did glide.

Right before lunch, Mary was concerned for safety,
    when her brothers and I, enjoying the packed snow,
decided to go one last time…together on one sled,
    to see how far and how fast we could go.

Bob lay down on his stomach on the sled first, followed
    by John, Phil, myself, and then Chris was on top.
Bob steered…we descended, picking up speed,
    and when we hit the mound…up we all did pop.

Our bodies were stacked in the air before we dropped,
    watching, Mary did flinch,
our combined weight squashed Bob against the sled,
    we moved…not another inch.

We all rose up on our feet…Bob was okay,
    fortunately, even the sled was not broken,
we had a good laugh over the incident,
    and went in to lunch then.

TR

149

February 20, 1981

October Moon

Len the 3rd lit his way to the barn by lantern
    under a full October moon.
To enjoy moonlit wanderings he'd learn
    and atop Ol' Dan he'd be soon.

Len guided Ol' Dan from his stall,
    a light workhorse colored black.
Len led Ol' Dan out into the crisp air of fall
    and climbed up on bareback.

Over the dirt roads Len would guide the horse,
    through the fields the lad would set course.
Riding at night gave Len solitude
    and would conjure up a contemplative mood.

Ol' Dan's ears would perk up from screech owl whistles
    while moving through tall grass and prickly thistles.
Len would sight deer through his mind's windows,
    flicks of white tails…into the shadows.

Hoohoohoo…hoohoohoo,
    concealed in the thicket was a great horned owl.
Len and Ol' Dan would walk on by
    but it wasn't safe for pheasant nor fowl.

Riding Ol' Dan up on Manuncachunk cliff,
    the Delaware River valley Len could see,
inhaling the fresh air with a whiff,
    the essence of nature's purity set Len free.

TR

February 15, 1981

<u>Orange Orb</u>

A quiet summer evening at Lac Landron,
    to the camp's kitchen came the voice of Rosco.
Last of the supper campfire's embers still did glow,
    Rosco beckoned me with something to show.

Out on the eastern horizon,
    was a long orange sliver.
Rosco and I peered out through the trees,
    coolness of night air caused me to shiver.

Optically, the moon arose above the far off foliage,
    became a brilliant orange orb.
Rosco and I could appreciate the view,
    our attention the full moon did absorb.

Lunar light awashed the landscape with its beam
    and streaked across the calm lake like a seam.
Breathing in fresh air made me feel hale,
    the moon rose higher and the color did pale.

TR

Our Weekly Agenda – Jess Reed, Beth Ann and Cathy Rue.

April 18, 2008

Our Weekly Agenda

Greg and Kathy Reed, friends of ours, have provided
    hearth and home for our daughters,
Cat had her own room while her sister Beth Ann
    shared with their friend Jess Reed living quarters.

Jess, Beth Ann and Cat attended together
    Northampton Community College in 2006-2007,
the close proximately of the Reed home
    in Nazareth was a handy convenience then.

The girls studied hard and each were inducted into
    the National Honor Society of Phi Beta Kappa.
But to break up study routine they had their special
    TV shows that Cat called 'our weekly agenda'.

While doing homework on any given weekday night
    Jess searched for Cat within sight,
whether in her room or elsewhere, then she'd recite,
    "Guess what show is on tonight?!"

"Wait! Don't tell me…yesterday
    was the Gauntlet," Cat would say,
"Tomorrow is America's Next Top Model,"
    excitedly she was bursting to tell.

"That makes tonight Tuesday…," exclaimed Cat,
    "which means American Idol is on!"
The girls would stop doing their homework,
    taking their daily study break was the reason.

For about an hour Jess, Beth Ann and Cat
    settled downstairs to watch TV.
Chitchat was interaction while watching their show,
    dessert was provided by Kathy.

Kathy made for them frozen mocha lattes
    or cake along with ice tea.
Once the show was over the three friends
    separated back to their individual study.

TR

Over Calm Water – Lac Landron.

March 7, 1982

Over Calm Water

As a lad staring out between the trees,
 a love I could feel,
I pondered the beginning and the end
 and onward a breeze did steal.

She was the epitome of my dreams,
 my heart was tapped.
upon the lake the wind created seams,
 over calm water it lapped.

For her to love me made me wonder,
 her strength I sought to reciprocate
but what disturbed the calm caused me ponder…
 what factors could I implicate.

She nourished my body and soul,
 helped me to root and grow,
I supported her as a towering white pine,
 branching out to bestow.

What direction did she take?...
 I peered at the disturbed surface,
she's lost among the current,
 the image faded of her face.

I looked towards the far shore,
 entrapped in searching is my spirit
for the love that needed a future
 as water escaped through the exit.

Understanding I beseeched futilely,
 it cleared through my glance
with wishing and hope receding,
 I recognized the lake's entrance.

Clearly…it was not love lost then
 with awareness of reentering reality.
It was a love that had not yet been
 …a love yet to be.

TR

April 26, 2006

Paddles and Garbage Can Lids

My family was living at Silve's, south of Millbrook
 in the early summer of 1967,
I was a lanky boy of twelve years,
 my brother Jim was then ten.

Our father, Len Rue was a naturalist and had departed
 on a summer-long photographic safari,
Jim and I either fought or played together a lot
 …when a mischievous idea came to me.

I proposed to Jim that we gather all of Dad's paddles
 into two equal piles,
we could be warriors and play war using them
 as spear-like wooden projectiles.

I suggested that we use garbage can lids
 to serve each of us as a shield.
The yard in front of the Silve's long porch
 would be our battlefield.

Jim readily agreed to participate and piled
 his paddles at the end of the driveway,
I stacked my 'spears' near the porch steps
 preparing for the fray.

I tried holding a garbage can lid
 and two paddles in my left grip
but my hand was not big enough,
 from my grasp the paddles did slip.

Jim and I faced each other when ready,
 waiting like warriors of old,
with raised shields and poised spears
 for the action to unfold.

"Go!" I signaled with a shout, which did impel
      thrown paddles...and about the yard
we ran in a rapid pell-mell,
      dodging projectiles that did bombard.

Thrown paddles were sought from the ground,
      retrieved to be reused when found,
those whose aim was well directed
      the garbage can lids handily deflected.

I ran...threw a paddle...then myself
      down behind our sea green colored canoe,
which provided temporary protection
      but removed Jim's location from view.

Where was Jim...I wondered that
      and raised my head to check,
eyes widened...a paddle thrown flat
      flew straight towards my neck.

I immediately ducked just in time...felt
      the paddle slide across my head,
quickly realizing if it had struck my neck
      I would now probably be dead.

From my prone position behind the canoe
      I called out for a truce,
since the close call of my neck being crushed
      did promptly induce.

A truce my brother readily agreed to,
      I rose up from behind the canoe,
we discussed what happened...had a good laugh
      but decided that enough was enough.

Having neither sustained no bodily injury
      nor cracked any paddles...we were lucky.
The instruments of war were put in place proper,
      with no one else the wiser.

TR

Pappy Dalrymple's Cane-back Rocker –
Benny Dalrymple and Beth Castner.

January 30, 1981

Pappy Dalrymple's Cane-back Rocker

The high cane-back rocker sat in the corner
    next to the wood burning stove.
It was a furnishing of Benny Dalrymple's,
    the corner was his own personal cove.

It was his throne in his home
    as he slowly rocked back and forth,
Benny mused over life in summer or winter
    with cold winds blowing out of the north.

When small Beth did something wrong
    such as kicking brother Lewis in the shin
she'd run for safety to her Pappy's chair
    so she wouldn't get a spankin'.

Pappy would hide Beth behind his chair,
    safe from her mother's wrath,
he wouldn't allow Alice to spank his granddaughter
    and was an obstacle in her path.

One day when Beth was seven
    Pappy no longer made the rocker sway
and she lost her corner sanctuary
    when he quietly passed away.

To the present Alice contends
    that the reason that Beth's always been sassy
was that she wasn't punished enough as a girl
    that was due a spunky lassie.

TR

160

December 3, 2006

Peril in Pittsburgh

Spring Break 1973…Chad and I had plans
    to hitchhike from Buckhannon to Clarksburg,
and catch a bus to where we would meet
    my friend's family in Pittsburgh.

After Humanities Class, on March 9, Chad and I
    departed the West Virginia Wesleyan campus,
backpacking through the town started our journey
    to walk the 12 miles to reach our bus.

In Buckhannon, two girls in a car stopped
    and asked us where we were going.
We told them Clarksburg and were offered a ride,
    thankfully…riding was better than walking.

Arriving in Clarksburg earlier than expected,
    Chad and I each purchased a ticket.
I played my harmonica while awaiting our bus,
    hopefully…not creating a racket.

Traveling on our bus was a mother and child,
    she seemed weary and harried,
I noticed there was no ring on her third finger
    indicating that she was not married.

Her bright-eyed young son's attention focused
    on my harmonica with rapt intent.
As an act of kindness I then gave my harmonica
    to the boy as a present.

Chad and I arrived in Pittsburgh
    hours before we were expected.
We walked around the park and waterfront
    where the three rivers are connected.

The confluence of the Allegheny and Monongahela
    forms the Ohio River with a steady flow,
between the Great Lakes and the Allegheny mountains
    Pittsburgh sits atop the Allegheny Plateau.

In 1754 the French built Fort Duquesne
    at the present Pittsburgh site,
but blew it up during the French and Indian War
    before that area fell to the British without a fight.

The British constructed Fort Pitt there and named it after
    their Secretary of State William Pitt the Elder.
Pittsburgh, named on April 22, 1794, was where boats
    were built aiding Ohio country settlers to enter.

Along the Monongahela, as darkness descended,
    Chad and I settled on a park bench,
off to our left the Ohio River began
    with the Allegheny joining as a branch.

On Pittsburgh's North Side, near Three Rivers Stadium,
    was displayed the creative, neon Westinghouse sign.
A row of encircled Ws, each underscored with a dash,
    lit up the night, with the number of Ws totaling nine.

Different sequences lit up each perimeter, W or dash,
    then blacked out…repeatedly restarted to flash.
I studied the lighting to detect a pattern…
    but a recurring sequence I could not discern.

A group of young people appeared off to our left,
    moved from the confluence of the rivers
and walked along the Monongahela in front of us
    as noisy, rowdy, rambunctious revelers.

The group walked beyond us off to our right,
    then moved forward to the river's edge.
I could hear people daring someone to jump
    into the water from the ledge.

Splash! Someone actually jumped into the cold water
        to experience some illogical thrill?
The group immediately ran off weaving back and forth,
        leaving their companion in peril.

As a body the group disappeared into the town.
        "Come back!" Chad and I heard voices shout.
We realized that whoever was in the water could drown
        since on their own they could not climb out.

Chad and I rushed to where we heard the voices call,
        found two panicked, young men below the wall,
grabbed their flailing arms…pulled them from the water,
        up onto the ledge where they were now safer.

The two wet men did not acknowledge their rescue,
        including not even saying a, "Thank you."
Stoned? They rushed off haphazardly and disoriented,
        in the direction their group had previously departed.

Shortly after this Chad and I retrieved our backpacks,
        I looked at the Westinghouse sign with a last view.
We then returned to the bus station where I would meet
        Chad's parents and sister at our rendezvous.

I spent an enjoyable weekend with Chad's family
        before continuing on with my journey,
to take a bus from Pittsburgh to Easton, PA,
        one step closer to home in Belvidere, New Jersey.

TR

December 29, 2007

Phone Service

Alexander Graham Bell invented the telephone in 1876.
    Through efforts by Dr. W.G. Cummins initially,
the West Jersey Toll telephone line was extended in 1896,
    into Warren County, New Jersey…finally.

The West Jersey Telephone Company set up shop
    between 314 and 318 on Front Street in Belvidere,
in a 2-story, red brick building amidst a row of businesses,
    adjacent to Yock's shoe store there.

Gertrude was born to Clint and Blanche Young Hartung
    on March 28, 1921, and when she was four or three
her parents installed a telephone in their Roxburg home,
    in the area theirs was the first and only.

The Hartungs could call to Belvidere unimpeded
    but could not reach Phillipsburg,
their service ended at the home of Dr. Harry Bossard,
    in Harmony Township, south of Roxburg.

Dr. Harry B. Bossard and his wife Jennie
    resided in their hillside residence in Harmony,
at the corner of the Hutchison Station Road
    and the Belvidere Phillipsburg Pike, I'm told.

When Blanche wanted to talk to someone in Phillipsburg
    she'd call Jennie Bossard who would relay
the message on, then Jennie would relay the answer
    back to Blanche, until everyone had their say.

Edith Vannatta Cook was married to Sam Cook,
    to Sam Cook…Van Y. was a brother,
Van was married to Jenny Hartung…and Jenny,
    to Blanche and Clint was a daughter.

Phone Service – Blanche and Clint Hartung.

Edith was a nighttime operator on Front Street,
    it could be quite quiet…she was all alone,
sometimes she'd hear a noise outside startling her,
    scared…she'd call Blanche up by telephone.

Awakened…Blanche would answer the ringing phone,
    discovered that noises in the night
had upset Edith…so they would converse
    until both were sure all was alright.

In 1933 when Gertrude was twelve, government agents,
    popular slang termed each a 'revenuer',
came to the Hartung home on the Belvidere Phillipsburg
    Pike and the Grist Mill Road corner.

On January 16, 1920, the 18th Constitutional Amendment
    outlawed the manufacture, sale, or transportation meant
for illegal liquor, called Prohibition but on December 5, 1933
    the 21st Amendment repealed the 18th in its entirety.

Logistical planning for a raid the revenuers did seek,
    upon the Roxburg Mill resting on Ragged Ridge Creek,
the source of water power for grinding grist into flour,
    now reputed to be the site of manufacturing illegal liquor.

On this site Captain Joseph and Margret Wilhelm Mackey
    built a grist mill prior to the American Revolution.
Joseph was Scotch-Irish and descended from the MacKay
    Highland Clan, and Blanche's ancestor as identification.

Joseph was born April 12, 1741, to William, in Harmony,
    his grandparents were John and Susannah Mackey.
Margret Wilhelm was born in 1742 in Londonderry, Ireland,
    married Joseph on May 4, 1762 in Sussex County.

Joseph sired with Margret eleven children starting with
    John born in 1763, then Joseph, William, and more
Elizabeth, Mary, Jeremiah, James, Lewis, Margaret, Richard,
    lastly Sarah Mackey Hazlitt born November 29, 1784.

Their home with small, high windows on the southern side
and standard-sized windows in front could be defended
from Indian attack by Joseph and the slaves housed
in barracks between the house and mill...once detected.

During the Revolution Joseph was commissioned a Captain
of Company 1, 1st Regiment of Militia of Sussex County,
on June 6, 1777, then was stationed under Brigadier General
William Winds at Elizabethtown with the army.

Captain Mackey's regiment was busy arresting Tories
in Sussex County during the year 1778,
if a jury found a Tory had joined or aided the British
then the confiscation of his property was his fate.

Margret operated the mill with the help of a devoted slave
while continuing to raise her large family,
and she maintained their home while Joseph was away,
keeping the mill running helped feed the army.

Before the war ended her two eldest sons, John and Joseph
served as privates in the Continental Army.
In 1780, Joseph Sr.'s regiment served in the Minisink area.
Militia of New Jersey was discharged November 31, 1783.

Joseph returned from the war, operated the mill profitably.
Margret died May 19, 1787, Joseph remarried a widow,
Rachel Hendershot on March 10, 1788, whose daughter
Hannah married Joseph's 3rd son William also.

The Presbyterian Church of Oxford, founded 1729, at Hazen
was where Margret was buried, and later Joseph when.
Her epitaph: She was a tender Mother, an Indulgent Wife,
reflected a family's testimony to her life.

Joseph died on October 12, 1798 as a prosperous miller,
the Mackeys operated the mill into the 19th century.
Christian Cressman bought the mill property in 1837,
due to the mill's age, he rebuilt a stone structure solidly.

About 1919 Mr. E. Leo Lommason bought and modernized
    the mill by removing the 40-foot millwheel, adding
a turbine and an auxiliary steam engine…but unprofitable
    for flour so illegal whiskey he began producing.

A written order was submitted to Clint and Blanche allowing
    agents access to the only phone in the community.
In order for the raid to be executed successfully
    Clint and Blanche were sworn to secrecy.

One night Clint and Blanche were at the Roxburg Grange,
    Gertrude, her brother Stuart, other neighboring children
were at the Hartungs…an explosion erupted!
    Everyone came over from the Grange then.

The raid commenced with the blowing up of the still
    at the whiskey producing mill that was modernized.
The revenuers ended the profitable operation at the mill
    and E. Leo Lommason was penalized.

Revenuers broke open the barrels releasing the booze,
    down Grist Mill Road it flowed…and stunk,
crossed the pike, into the Hartung roadside barn it did ooze,
    the cows lapped up the liquor and became drunk.

TR

January 22, 1981

Pink Sky

It was early summer at Lac Landron,
    I saw the sky with a blink.
I scurried over evergreen needles to see,
    the radiance was brilliant pink.

I decided to watch and settled down
    into a spruce tree trunk's crook.
Pink reflected off the smooth lake surface
    as I viewed from ol' Charley's nook.

Jutting upwards into the pink sky
    rose pine and spruce spires,
silhouetted and mirrored upon the lake
    was a view that inspires.

Pink faded to lavender…to purple,
    evening coolness of spruce I did scent.
Purple to indigo…to black of night,
    stars sparkling in the firmament.

TR

February 3, 1981

Pose for Pictures

Scotty and the gang headed north
    on a Canadian jaunt,
they decided to stop enroute for refreshments
    at a roadside restaurant.

As the gang went through a cafeteria line
    Scotty noticed that the counter girl was sulky,
by using his camera he'd enliven her spirits,
    "My, you sure are pretty."

"I'd like to take your picture," Scotty said,
    "You see I work for Teen Magazine."
The girl's face shone with a beam
    and for the pictures she began to preen.

Scotty had the girl pose this way and that,
    the girl showed continual smiles.
Scotty told her she took a good photo
    causing the girl to display feminine wiles.

Scotty and the gang sat down to snack,
    the girl maintained a hopeful glance.
The gang enjoyed her attention as she thought
    perhaps this was her big chance.

Prior to departing on towards their destination
    Scotty thanked the girl for her cooperation,
"If we stop here on the way back from Canada
    I'll have to put film in the camera."

The girl's face registered surprise…
    then vexation.
Scotty and the gang departed…
    without hesitation.

TR

June 30, 2006

<u>Put On the 'peed Daddy</u>

Dust billowed up from the dry, dirt road,
 which was muddy in spots when rainy,
a trail widened by feet, horse and wagon,
 then traversed by the Ford Model T.

The brook tumbled…pooled…cascaded down
 alongside and crossed underneath the dirt road,
which weaved itself up through Lommason Glen,
 dotted here and there with a human abode.

Trees and shrubs covered the steep slopes,
 plants down along the babbling brook,
such as Jack-in-the-pulpit and trailing arbutus,
 prompted people to take a closer look.

Each 'Jack' or spadix in Jack-in-the-pulpit
 was covered by a spathe, a large hooded bract,
but it was the aromatic trailing arbutus
 that caused people to irresponsibly act.

In spring the town people drove to the glen to dig up
 the blooming trailing arbutus for transplant,
due to its delicate, little, white, trumpet flowers so fragrant,
 now prohibited in many areas to protect this plant.

The road rose up by the Hornbakers, Matthews, Ouellettes
 on the left…and off to the right was a driveway,
rising to where Beth's great grandparents Daniel and Jane
 Dalrymple lived, on a hill, until in 1913 both passed away.

Beth Castner's neighbors were her childhood friends,
 including the Hornbaker girls named Joyce and Lois,
George Ouellette and Al Sweet, who played together
 year-round, of which she did fondly reminisce.

Put on the 'peed Daddy – Lommason Glen.

Beth's small two-story house stood on the hill
    at the Lommason Glen Road intersection,
driving straight eastward it became Buckhorn Drive,
    Summerfield Road turned in a northward direction.

Buckhorn Drive ascended up beyond Castner Road,
    curving left past the Owl's Nest the road turned,
on by the possible homestead of pioneer Jacob Rush,
    looping back to Summerfield Road it returned.

In 1930 Beth was four and lived with her parents
    Lew and Alice Castner, grandfather Benny Dalrymple,
sister Jessie Mae, brother Lewis and cousin Alice Cruts,
    ensconced in the small home populated with people.

Alice Cruts, Alice's niece was five when she came
    in 1914, to live with her aunt's family,
after her father, Elmer had died, her mother Nettie
    couldn't keep her family together financially.

Alice Cruts assisted with Beth, her young cousin,
    helping her dress as part of her care,
and tied bows of bright, colorful ribbon
    in the little girl's whitish blond hair.

Beth's family would prepare for church attendance
    at Summerfield…since it was a Sunday,
except for Benny who preferred to stay home,
    making his cane-back rocker sway.

The M. E. Church of Scott's Mountain was built in 1836,
    part of the 1800s burgeoning Methodist denomination,
became the Summerfield M. E. Church when rebuilt in 1857.
    Alice, as a girl of 12, in 1906 joined this congregation.

Church services were at two o' clock P.M. on Sundays,
    since Summerfield shared a pastor with Oxford.
The pastor preached at Oxford on Sunday mornings,
    one was what two small congregations could afford.

Put on the 'peed Daddy –
Alice Cruts, Jessie Mae, Lewis and Beth Castner.

Each Sunday morning was a quick, busy time,
  Beth's family would eat a small lunch,
but Alice would precook meat and potatoes
  for a large supper feast after church.

Bright ribbons adorned the girls' hair while Alice
  wore a hat, each were bedecked in a dress,
Lew and his son Lewis wore Sunday suits to church,
  and both were usually hatless.

Lew and William Hornbaker were the first residents
  to buy motorized vehicles up Lommason Glen,
William bought a Ford Model T truck while Lew
  purchased a Model T sedan, back in 1927.

From 1908 to 1927 the Ford Model T or 'Tin Lizzie'
  was produced by Henry Ford's Ford Motor Company,
and "put America on wheels" by being affordable
  due to production line ease to mass assemble.

Lew's black, enclosed, two-door sedan had two seats,
  gears of two speeds and reverse, rear wheel drive,
with 25-30 mpg, and when Henry made his 10 millionth car,
  9 out of 10 cars were Fords worldwide.

Lew would set the spark and throttle
  in a ten minutes to three position,
then he'd grip the crank in his right hand
  to turn clockwise initiating ignition.

With his left forefinger through the choke
  wire loop, Lew began pulling,
while simultaneously turning the crank
  until the car began rumbling.

Retard the spark or out of time turning
  was a cause for alarm…
a sudden, spinning kickback of the crank
  could break an arm.

Once started...to keep the car rumbling,
    Lew jumped to the running board,
turned the spark and throttle to a twenty five minutes
    to two position, on the puttering Ford.

Jessie Mae, Lewis and Alice Cruts entered the car,
    into the back seat they squeezed,
Beth sat in front between her parents or on her Mom's lap,
    down the angled driveway the Model T eased.

Past the Bischoffs and the Sweets Lew drove
    on the Summerfield Road providing straight access.
While Beth was four there was a temporary time
    she could not pronounce the letter 's'.

As the Model T began to scale the incline,
    Beth wanted the car to go quick,
and would often say, "Put on the 'peed Daddy,
    'o we don't 'tick."

Lew would chuckle at this pronouncement,
    of his daughter aged four,
the Model T moved faster beginning its ascent
    while he pressed on the accelerator.

The road became steeper as it approached near
    the top...Lew changed gear,
Johnson's Farm, a family run resort was over the rise,
    the enterprise was viewed with passengers' eyes.

The Johnson family started out with a bed and breakfast,
    after having immigrated from Denmark,
they expanded with cottages, hosting company picnics,
    a pool, and left on their community their mark.

Summerfield Road dipped down past the Johnson home,
    then rose in a quick, second peak,
the dirt road descended with the mountain church in view,
    where of Jesus Christ the pastor would speak.

Buckhorn Drive reconnected with the Summerfield Road,
    just below the church painted white,
Lew parked opposite the church or along the lane
    running back to the cemetery within sight.

The dust cloud slowly settled onto the vacant road,
    once the Model T rumbled on by,
like precious memories of a passing…bygone era
    saying a reluctant, "Goodbye."

TR

May 12, 2009

Questions

Cathy performed her student teaching in a couple
    of inner city schools
as part of her Kutztown University teaching training
    of experience and using educational tools.

Cathy was assigned at one inner city school,
    to teach fourth grade was the intent.
One day in a class populated mostly by minorities,
    she was approached by a Hispanic student.

"Ms. Rue, do you have a boyfriend?" Jose asked.
    "No," Cathy did cite.
Jose pulled his small, clenched fist backwards
    and happily declared, "Alright!"

A few days later Jose again approached Cathy.
    "Ms. Rue, are you married?" he wanted to know.
Cathy replied, "No." Jose inquired further,
    "Do you have kids?" Cathy replied, "No."

Jose continued his questions, "How old are you?"
    Cathy responded, "Twenty-two."
Jose exclaimed, "And you don't have any kids?!"
    Here's peeking at an inner city cultural view?

TR

Reliable Watchdog – Len Rue, Jr. and Rusty.

July 26, 1981

Reliable Watchdog

Rusty was the family pet,
  a spaniel called a clumber,
at Camp Pahaquarra before the doorway
  he would curl and slumber.

It was late one night when Dad finished
  working in his upstairs' darkroom.
He stepped out onto an exterior balcony,
  high above stars did loom.

Dad descended the stairway steep,
  adorned without a railing.
The noise awakened Rusty from sleep,
  from his throat came growling.

Rusty rose up from his curl,
  peering into the dark,
towards the intruder the dog did hurl,
  alarming with his bark.

Dad turned the corner…both were surprised,
  his master Rusty then recognized.
Quickly Rusty ran past to the porch's edge,
  barked off from the concrete ledge.

Toward an unseen rival Rusty did bay,
  Dad watched the dog facing away,
Rusty's sheepish glance back exposed his mistake
  and interrupted his deploying fake.

Dad thought the incident humorous
  due to the antics of the animal,
but Rusty was a reliable watchdog
  that befits a clumber spaniel.

TR

180

February 28, 1982

Russian Spy

In the early 1960s, Sean worked as a chemist,
    utilizing his doctorate in chemistry,
for a company doing confidential government work,
    located in northern New Jersey.

Sean had two subordinates in his lab,
    each was a chemist and an American,
while one was a native the other was naturalized
    with origins of being a Russian.

Nicolai considered himself a Ukrainian,
    not a detested Red Russian,
he claimed the Reds killed his family
    and he fled as a refugee.

Nicolai fled the U.S.S.R. through Europe,
    came to America then,
encountered and married a Chinese girl,
    became a U.S. citizen.

Q & G are the initials of a company's name,
    shortened and changed to preserve identity,
that hired Nicolai as a chemist,
    giving him work in their laboratory.

Q & G's good recommendation aided Nicolai past security,
    stressing that he was anti-communist.
Nicolai applied and was hired in Sean's department
    and worked a few years as a chemist.

One early morning after Nicolai had been employed,
    summoned by Ken, the chief of security,
were Sean and the other chemist named Herman,
    for them someone waited to see.

Inside was a man neither did recognize
    who was from the F.B.I.,
and the agent revealed to all a surprise
    that Nicolai could be a Russian spy.

At an American-Russian track meet
    held earlier that year,
agents noticed that every time a Russian won
    Nicolai would enthusiastically cheer.

Copies of lab documents also surfaced in Russia,
    one of our spies reported,
these originated from Sean's company's laboratory
    and F.B.I. concerns were supported.

Only those in the room would know,
    the F.B.I. sought their cooperation
to be alert and report Nicolai's actions,
    they'd catch him relaying information.

To cooperate with the F.B.I.
    Sean, Herman and Ken did agree.
Sean noticed that Ken who's strongly anti-communist,
    was full of glee.

One evening as two F.B.I. men held surveillance,
    Nicolai exited his home in a suburb
and entered his car carrying copied documents,
    was followed away from the curb.

Observing Nicolai drive up to a parked car,
    in the parking lot of a supermarket,
the F.B.I. took pictures of the exchange,
    to two men Nicolai handed a packet.

Nicolai drove away from the scene,
    the other spies' departure was quick
and in the ensuing car chase
    spies eluded agents in traffic.

Without material evidence Nicolai remained free,
    so the F.B.I. continued their surveillance
hoping to catch his contacts with documents
    in another future chance.

But to retain Nicolai in a confidential lab
    was too risky the F.B.I. then decided,
directing that clearance be lifted with no reason given,
    to Ken and Sean they confided.

One morning while working in his office
    Sean heard a disturbance,
Ken and another had come for Nicolai
    to lift his security clearance.

Gripping each arm the security men
    removed Nicolai from the lab physically,
led the spy forcefully down the hall,
    Ken performed his duty happily.

Ken told Nicolai that his clearance was taken away,
    he'd have no job after today,
under escort his personal belongings he could retrieve,
    out the gate he'd be forced to leave.

Nicolai was escorted back to gather his items,
    he burst through Sean's door,
being visibly upset he professed ignorant innocence,
    Sean thought, "What an actor."

A reason for dismissal Nicolai did demand
    stating he did not understand,
Sean said that clearance was removed by the F.B.I.
    and they do not have to say why.

"Is there anything you can do?" pleaded Nicolai,
    "It's beyond my control," Sean responded why,
"Challenge the F.B.I.'s decision if you want,
    if you think it does warrant."

Subsequently, with Nicolai knowing the law was near
    he did suddenly disappear.
His home, wife and life he abandoned
    to avoid possibly being imprisoned.

The theory was that Nicolai fled to Russia,
    nowhere was he to be seen,
given false identity papers he escaped
    by airline or by submarine?

Sean told his colleagues about Nicolai
    having spied in their laboratory,
they were surprised and reluctant
    to believe the spy story.

A few months later one of Sean's colleagues
    traveled to the U.S.S.R.
as part of an American group to participate
    in a science seminar.

On a Moscow street one day the colleague saw
    Nicolai coming his way,
but Nicolai stopped when spotting the colleague
    and quickly ran away.

In the mid-1960s Sean's company closed,
    westward their operations were transferred,
he remained and was hired by a local company
    since staying in this area he preferred.

Going to a seminar in the early 70s,
    to Q & G's representative Sean said, "Hi."
Sean inquired of the man if he had known Nicolai,
    the representative replied, "Oh…the Russian spy."

The F.B.I. sought to remove Nicolai
    because of secrets they knew he stole,
but based on Q & G's good recommendation…
    hmmm…had there been any ethical violation?

TR

January 19, 1981

Security Guard

The man is out on his round
    providing customer security,
adorned with a silver badge
    limiting companies' liability.

Quiet…it is through the night,
    stands the guard all alone.
He awaits the crack of morning light
    and a cup of coffee he may hone.

Carrying about him a time clock,
    he checks each important lock.
Traversing the warehouse and the yard
    walks on the security guard.

TR

November 14, 1981

Seeking the Plum Tree

I worked odd jobs when growing up near Millbrook,
    during summers cast hot and sunny,
labored for an elderly Russian widow Mrs. Mordkin,
    to earn for myself some money.

Mrs. Mordkin interrupted our work of clearing brush
    one humid, late afternoon,
to speak to me while I grew anxious
    to be heading homeward soon.

Mrs. Mordkin talked to me about her friend,
    a neighbor of long ago,
I hoped her story wouldn't last long,
    swimming I planned to go.

Mrs. Mordkin told me about neighbors
    who held her friend in low regard,
due to her family's rough reputation,
    and life for her was hard.

When the Mordkins came to this valley
    the first neighbor who opened home and heart
was her friend who lived down the road
    and a friendship had its start.

Mrs. Mordkin wanted to visit her neighbor's house,
    urging me to accompany,
and sensing that I was hesitant to agree,
    told me about the plum tree.

Mrs. Mordkin suggested we go for plums
    in order to entice,
I agreed to accompany upon deciding
    a plum would taste nice.

Down an overgrown road once the main thoroughfare
    Mrs. Mordkin and I walked with care
due to her legs requiring time to take
    and my eyes wary for any snake.

We stopped off to the right of the road
    before an overgrown yard,
to observe the wooden structure of an abandoned abode
    and the desolation due to disregard.

In front of the house stood a sentinel,
    a branching solitary tree,
my eyes searched in amongst the leaves,
    no fruit could I see.

I inquired of Mrs. Mordkin if this was the plum tree
    belonging to her past neighbor,
but her concentration was centered elsewhere
    while telling me she wasn't sure anymore.

I gazed at her profile being baffled,
    but then I caught a stime,
my mind comprehended our quest's true purpose
    to seek another place in time.

I asked if she'd like to approach the house near,
    despite the unknown causing a fear,
but Mrs. Mordkin declined the offer to go there
    saying she could view from here.

I thought this might be Mrs. Mordkin's last visit
    due to age afflicting fate,
so I stepped back to allow unencumbered remembrance...
    for her departure I'd silently wait.

TR

February 6, 2006

Sharon

In Belvidere's Methodist Church on April 16, 1981
    Mary and I were married,
she encouraged our involvement with Country Gate Players,
    and I eventually agreed.

We acted in bit parts of different plays,
    our first was a musical entitled Shenandoah,
Mary played as a Southern Belle,
    a Confederate soldier was my persona.

Other plays in which one or both of us participated were
    Guys and Dolls, Carousel, The Pirates of Penzance,
The Sound of Music, 1776, The Music Man,
    each involved singing and/or choreographed dance.

In December 1983 prior to the holidays,
    Mary and I received an invitation
to a party sponsored by Country Gate Players,
    held at Belvidere's American Legion.

The invitation had stated to come as you may,
    maybe as a character from a past play,
perhaps a pirate, Keystone Cop, Dr. Josiah Bartlett for me,
    or a nun, Austrian countess, Hot Box dancer for Mary.

I decided to dress conservatively
    in my pinstripe, gray suit,
A light blue taffeta gown on Mary
    did elegantly suit.

Mary decided to attend characterized as Sharon,
    from our personalized, recurring role-playing game,
bedecked in a blonde wig she then became
    this sexy, sophisticated dame.

Sharon – Mary Rue.

Sharon's trademark was her hair colored blonde,
  of her being uninhibited I was quite fond,
blond stars Jean Harlow, Marilyn Monroe and Sandra Dee
  reminded me of my wild lady.

For Mary's role sexy undergarments were worn,
  stockings and a garter belt did adorn,
encasing her feet high heeled white shoes were upon,
  which completed the ensemble of Sharon.

Sharon and I arrived ready to socialize…
  seeing us registered some surprise?
There was an awkwardness I could apprise
  and felt upon us many eyes.

As we approached friends as a couple
  they all seemed to shy away,
this was making us uncomfortable,
  confused feelings did not allay.

Sharon and I ended up standing alone,
  the reason was not known,
but the intentional isolation we did perceive…
  pondered that we should leave.

As Sharon and I conversed alone
  Ellie approached us quite wary,
squinted as she studied cautiously,
  "My…is that you Mary?"

We answered, "Yes."…Ellie resounded with glee
  at discovering Mary's identity,
and stated that it was the wig that Mary wore
  as to why she was not sure.

Our fellow thespians were informed by Ellie
  as to Mary's true identity,
they began to gather around us quickly,
  a nagging thought came to me…

Now that Mary's identity was recognized
    we were warmly greeted,
but they'd thought I had brought some else I surmised
    and of my wife I'd cheated.

I was tired when we arrived home late
    but circumstances and attire acted as foreplay,
Sharon was aggressively amorous and being a gentleman
    …I let her have her way.

TR

November 29, 1981

<u>Sleepy Dust</u>

Earlier this year on April 25th
 the morning's approaches softly tread,
I scurried with preparations in the kitchen,
 served Mary breakfast in bed.

Mary finished eating propped up in bed
 and with light of an overcast, grayish tint,
I observed her attired in a beige nightie,
 she suddenly began to squint.

I watched Mary rubbing her eyes above
 the curvature of her covered bust,
and upon inquiring about what she was doing
 she replied, "…removing sleepy dust."

To show me her technique I requested as a tease
 and she sought to please,
she squinted above soft cheeks resembling a cherub,
 her fingers began to rub.

Simultaneously from her eyelashes she wiped
 the gritty particles of small size,
I enjoyed her earnest demonstration
 of clearing her blue eyes.

TR

July 10, 2005

Stinky Feet

As I sat on our couch in September 1992
    beside me was Beth Ann sharing a seat,
my daughter was only four and a half,
    when she said, "Smell my feet."

I did not want to smell her stinky feet,
    and did so vocally deem,
Beth Ann smiled and told me
    her feet smelled like ice cream.

Had she stepped in something that smelled good?
    I decided to take a sniff,
leaned over and pulled her one foot up
    and took a deep whiff.

Her foot stunk. "You have stinky feet,"
    I said on the matter,
Beth Ann, having tricked me,
    rocked with raucous laughter.

TR

April 8, 2006

Stranded by a Snake

Camp Pahaquarra, of the George Washington Council,
    was a Boy Scout camp where my Dad, Len,
worked as a ranger and we lived there year round until,
    in 1964 we moved to Silve's then.

Dad kept various animals for his naturalist work
    and for the camp's Nature Center while the ranger,
these included foxes, raccoons, skunks, snakes, etc.
    to us their presence was no stranger.

My brothers and I attended school in Blairstown and
    on one spring day of nineteen sixty one or sixty
an incident occurred when Dad visited a friend, Dick Zipzer,
    while domestic duties kept Beth, my Mom, busy.

Dick Zipzer was a New York printer who resided
    in the original Abraham Van Campen abode,
built prior to the French and Indian War
    on a bluff along the Old Mine Road.

Mom was busy washing the breakfast dishes,
    a movement caught her glance,
her eyes detected a reddish-brown colored serpent
    as it entered through the kitchen entrance.

The snake slithered across the kitchen floor
    …it was a copperhead!
It slithered directly towards Mom at the sink,
    she felt a feeling of dread.

Mom, in rubber gloves, moved away from the sink
    towards the horizontal freezer,
the snake changed direction pursuing her,
    she climbed up to avoid danger.

Stranded by a Snake – Milk Snake.

The snake slithered in under the freezer,
    Mom was stranded on the top then,
she didn't know where it was and couldn't step down,
    not wanting to be bitten.

Mom was stranded for hours on top
    of the horizontal appliance,
couldn't find the snake whichever way she'd glance
    and awaited Dad's assistance.

Dad returned from visiting Dick Zipzer
    to find Mom perched atop the freezer.
Chased by a copperhead…Mom told what did happen.
    …but she was mistaken.

Dad explained that it was not a copperhead
    but a nonpoisonous milk snake instead,
tan with a black-bordered reddish-brown blotched pattern
    prompts easy mistaken identity causing concern.

The milk snake was stored in a cardboard box,
    in Dad's office opposite the kitchen.
It was rambunctious and knocked over the box,
    escaping into the front hall then.

After giving reassurance Dad then helped Mom
    down from her perch.
He pulled the freezer out from the wall
    when conducting his search.

Behind the freezer a small hole was found
    along the baseboard near the floor,
conjecture was that the milk snake went through
    and was seen nevermore.

Told the snake tale after returning from school
    were Len, Jim and I,
thereafter when entering the kitchen…behind the freezer
    I kept a watchful eye.

TR

September 12, 1982

Tipped

In the poem <u>Uncoordinated Action</u>
    Brian and I continued our trek,
paddling down the channel of the Festebert,
    through the North Woods of Quebec.

The morning shone bright like expectant youth,
    I recently turned sixteen.
We paddled towards a destination entering a lake,
    surrounding shores crested with evergreen.

We traversed the lake and small isthmus
    entering Pikitakijuan Lake,
paddled for the channel opposite us,
    it did not long take.

Roar of the rapids ahead became louder,
    I wondered if we were late,
but portaging scouts blocked the shore momentarily
    so Brian and I drifted to wait.

I noticed submersed series of small, spherical sacs
    clinging to branches for support,
Brian said that bladders entrap food from passing current,
    belong to a bladderwort.

Upon beaching we lifted out our gear,
    portaged a half mile,
weaving a narrow, muddy trail wet with dew,
    to deposit packs in a pile.

We joined our companions watching rapids
    from huge shoreline boulders.
Observing the swiftness of the water
    we were fascinated beholders.

The last two canoes beached above the rapids,
    Kris joined Uncle Bill giving instruction
on zigzagging a course around the rocks,
    to avoid tipping and destruction.

Two huge boulders known as the Twins,
    foreboding in the scene,
set midstream near the end of the run
    which canoeists should pass in-between.

For our turn Brian and I ascended the trail,
    donned preservers to be prepared,
drifted in our canoe close to shore,
    for Kris's signal we stared.

Kris waved to us to descend,
    to paddle fast instructed Brian.
Brian steered our bow into the current's V,
    I paddled hard then.

On a wave's crest we rose,
    paddling straight we aimed,
downwards the bow dropped,
    against a rock we rammed!

The impact tossed me forward…I saw
    in the bow a cleft,
the bow hung against the rock
    but our stern was swept left.

Turning in my seat to paddle stern,
    my paddle I tightly gripped,
but the sweeping canoe shifted our weight,
    downstream our canoe tipped.

Brian escaped out of the canoe's path,
    but I was caught below
in the swirling of the rapids flow…
    I knew where to go.

While gripping my paddle I grabbed
    the approaching swamped canoe's rim,
dunked myself underneath the canoe,
    over my head the bottom did skim.

My head bobbed through the surface,
    I grabbed a gunnel handhold,
amidst shouts of jeers, cheers or fears,
    descending through rapids I rode.

I descended with my feet forward,
    bouncing over any submerged lump,
but bobbing about exposed my rump
    receiving an occasional posterior bump.

Towards the central Twin the canoe bore,
    its path I tried to detour
but could not brace to cause a veer
    as the boulder came more ominously near.

I released my handhold sparing a moment,
    against the Twin forced the current,
against the rock the canoe crushed,
    against the aluminum I was flushed.

I braced myself against the current,
    to loosen the canoe I decided to try,
slipped my fingers along the aluminum rim,
    strained upwards in an immobile pry.

I crawled onto the other rock…faced shore,
    called above the rapids roar
asking of what I should do of Uncle Bill,
    he hollered for me to stand still.

They were taking pictures of my predicament,
    conjuring a degree of embarrassment,
but I enjoyed the event of being a ham,
    photographically I am.

Tipped – Tim Rue in the Pikitakijuan Rapids, 1970.

Uncle Bill led a group of eight or seven,
  by interlocking arms they created a chain,
traversing from shore out into the current,
  distance they slowly did gain.

One scout moving along the chain slipped,
  losing his grip…he dipped,
he was swept away in the rapids flow,
  bobbed to the pool's surface below.

The group gathered above the Twin,
  gripped the canoe where current clenched,
pulled upwards on the rim in unison,
  from the rock face they wrenched.

The bent canoe was released in the rapids,
  into the pool it tumbled,
upon being instructed to drag it to shore,
  I complied feeling humbled.

Between the Twins I tossed myself,
  the current spit me forwards,
I hit the pool's surface below,
  near the canoe I swam towards.

I swam the swamped canoe to shore,
  handed an awaiting group an end,
they emptied out the water,
  placed it around a rock to rebend.

Brian met me as I climbed out
  and felt I was responsible for our mishap.
I explained that I had not seen the rock,
  Uncle Bill directed us to collect balsam sap.

I quickly moved to retrieve my Randall,
  stepped away from the rocky shore
leaving behind the lacerated, aluminum canoe,
  Brian followed me for the chore.

I scaled the nearby, steep hill,
    quickly on the double,
scanned the brush for a balsam fir
    covered with many a bubble.

Approaching a tree with dark gray, bubbly bark
    I slit tops of bubbles and collected
upon my knife's blade the sticky sap,
    our conversation continued I recollected.

I restated that I had not seen
    the rock…the wave had hidden,
continued collecting the balsam sap,
    a voice called for our return then.

Our canoe was reformed to proper shape
    with lacerations covered over by duct tape,
others applied around tape seams the balsam gum,
    I marveled over flexibility of aluminum.

Despite the patched and wrinkled appearance
    the canoe did float,
but some of our gear was redistributed
    so as not to overstrain the boat.

Brian and I could not shoot any other rapids
    due to usage being limited,
but for me the morning's events already beheld
    an Adventure Unlimited.

TR

April 1, 2006

Tit for Tat

About May 1980 Scotty, Homer, Alan and I decided
    to head north for a quick visit,
to Homer's cabins at Lac Landron, Quebec, Canada,
    we quickly planned for it.

We left after work on Wednesday,
    departing from Belvidere, New Jersey,
with plans to return on Sunday,
    to be back for work on Monday.

We reached Binghamton, New York at about
    ten to ten thirty at night,
and were hungry so we decided to stop
    for a quick bite.

We pulled over and entered a restaurant seeing
    one lone waitress behind the counter,
the place was devoid of other customers,
    we stepped forward to give her our order.

The young waitress had a large bosom,
    a nametag hung over her left breast,
of fast food we each ordered some
    planning to enjoy our quick rest.

As our orders were paid for and processed
    Scotty engaged the waitress in conversation,
her face brightened as they talked, then he
    asked her to guess his occupation.

She could not guess Scotty's occupation,
    not having enough info to suffice,
he then told the waitress that he operates
    a school bus service.

Scotty next turned the waitresses' attention
    to our fellow traveler named Alan,
she tried but could not guess the occupation
    of the tall, strapping, young man.

Scotty said that Alan had played football
    for a professional team,
but was not currently playing due to an injury,
    the waitress showed Alan an attentive gleam.

The waitress became very talkative with Alan,
    she must have been a football fan.
She was excited and evidently enamored,
    his attention was quite favored.

I stood off to the side
    silently watching the interaction.
"What do you think he does?" asked Scotty
    introducing in my direction.

Scotty had been calling me Levi Zendt,
    referring to a shunned, Mennonite character
from the televised miniseries Centennial,
    based on the 1974 book by James Michener.

A bushy beard, a broad brimmed felt hat colored green,
    and in a red plaid jacket I was seen.
Towards me the waitress' attention did divert,
    she loudly announced, "He's a sex pervert."

We all erupted with laughter,
    though at my expense.
I pensively pondered, "How would she know?
    Did she have a sixth sense?"

Alan looked at me, then leaned in pointing
    at her nametag, "That's the name of that one…"
He then pointed to her prominent right breast,
    "What's the name of the other one?"

The waitresses' mouth fell open in surprise...
    anger clouded her face,
we grabbed up our fast food
    and hastened from that place.

We recounted the incident with laughter
    after departing the restaurant,
proceeded towards the Thousand Islands Bridge
    on our Canadian jaunt.

The waitress knew how to dish it out,
    but could not take that,
it was a simple case of turnabout,
    it was...tit for tat.

TR

To Bed at Ten – John and Mary Van Nimwegen Sellner, 1936.

November 23, 2006

To Bed at Ten

Mae Sellner Rue, my grandmother, chuckled
    as she recounted this tale
of how her father, John Joseph Sellner, nightly,
    retired to bed at ten without fail.

John maintained this habit strictly
    while operating a grocery store and bakery,
at 1137 Main Street in Paterson, New Jersey,
    in the early twentieth century.

John, after closing his store in 1917,
    became a night watchman at a mill on Getty Avenue,
and was later accompanied by a German shepherd,
    provided by his son-in-law, Leonard Rue.

Mae said her mother, Mary Van Nimwegen Sellner,
    occasionally joked that John, her husband,
would have gone to bed at ten even if visited
    by Victoria, the Queen of England.

TR

December 17, 2006

Tons of Fun

About April 1980, a group including Homer, Scotty and I
    headed north to Canada for a four day vacation,
going to Homer's cabins up on Lac Landron, Quebec,
    for good company, rest and relaxation.

We drove into the clearing in front of Homer's quarters…
    garbage, including organic, was strewn about in view.
It was obvious the people standing there were squatters,
    and they were recognized as the…Tet de Boule.

The Tet de Boule is a clan of the Southern Cree,
    down from James Bay they had migrated,
onto Algonquin land, north of Maniwaki,
    their being 'bullheaded' often made others irritated.

The Tet de Boule just stood there watching us,
    as we surveyed the group I didn't see one man,
but there were a number of children of various ages,
    and one large bosomed, heavyset, Indian woman.

The stout Indian woman, of unknown age, with stringy,
    straight gray hair and a reddish-brown complexion,
wore a dirty plaid skirt and a greasy, light-blue T-shirt,
    and Scotty nicknamed her 'Tons of Fun'.

Homer spoke to 'Tons of Fun' about their squatting,
    meanwhile…Scotty took a profile picture only to find
that with Homer's left hand cupped and hanging outwards
    it looked like he was grabbing her behind.

We had caught them in the act of leaving winter quarters,
    moving onwards, they had already gotten a start.
They now were waiting for George, their clan leader,
    to come pick them and remaining stuff up, to depart.

When we checked the big cabin there was a surprise
    of the wood burning stove that we saw,
a fire had been built to burn sooooo hot,
    it actually split the cast iron wall.

Despite an outhouse not far from the big cabin,
    which served adequately its intent,
a bathtub in the side room of Homer's cabin
    was left with deposited excrement.

I noticed strips of dried moose meat hanging on a pole
    set back in, off to the left of Homer's cabin,
wandered over for a closer look, saw two 6-gallon
    Shell cans near the smoked meat, decided to look in.

Chunks of rotting moose meat were in both Shell cans,
    whitish colored maggots covered, infested the meat.
I asked one Indian boy why they left the meat there.
    He replied that the meat they were going to eat.

I made my way back over to Scotty to let him know
    what these Tet de Boule had to eat,
thought of the children possibly suffering,
    maybe sharing some food we could treat.

At one point, Scotty and I stood with our backs towards
    the woods, while he spoke with 'Tons of Fun',
about being responsible and cleaner, she stood there
    drinking a bottle of beer…then finished that one.

'Tons of Fun' tossed the empty bottle over our heads,
    into the woods…Scotty bid her to hear,
that doing that was bad…someone might step on it.
    She replied, "Don't worry…I won't go over there."

George, the leader of these Tet de Boule, and his brother,
    showed up with a pickup truck late in the day.
They began to load their belongings into the bay…
    I wondered where they might stay.

Before it was time to start preparing our supper meal,
    we made sandwiches of peanut butter on bread
and gave them to the Tet de Boule Indian clan
    until they were adequately fed.

George let Homer know if they needed a place to stay,
    usually when the weather turned wintry
and it is necessary to escape from the elements,
    that locks on doors would not prevent their entry.

Since no law was available to prevent access,
    Homer ended up giving the Tet de Boule a key,
with the deal being that they wouldn't leave a mess
    and to look after the property.

Occasionally, Scotty would pull out the profile picture,
    much to Homer's chagrin,
and teased that 'Tons of Fun' was being squeezed,
    contributing to many a grin.

TR

August 29, 1981

Torn Buttock

After Hitler attacked his Russian ally
    its Polish prisoners Russia freed.
From forced labor camps Poles were released,
    to be allies Russia agreed.

A Polish government was established in exile
    due to this time of trial,
Russia permitted formation of a Polish army
    with only materials for an infantry.

Technical people, pilots had no equipment in Russia
    so they were sent overland,
to embark seaward from Middle Eastern Persia
    and travel by ship to England.

Tomasz Rozvadowski was in his early twenties
    when the Pole was sent to Iran.
He was being shipped to England in late forty-one
    and to be a pilot was his plan.

Tomasz left Iran aboard a British ship.
    But the Nazi blocked the Suez,
so southward to round the Cape of Good Hope,
    along east Africa traveled Tomasz.

Near the cape off of South Africa
    against the ship something did explode.
The sinking ship prompted abandonment
    due to being torpedoed.

Tomasz found himself adrift in the ocean,
    he spotted a rubber raft
and swam towards it seeking it's safety
    leaving the sinking ship abaft.

As Tomasz's comrades pulled him into the raft
    up a shark did jump,
out of the ocean it lunged forward,
    its teeth grasped Tomasz's rump.

The shark jerked Tomasz in its grip,
    a chunk of flesh did rip.
The shark dropped into the ocean colored red
    from the inflicted wound that bled.

In the raft Tomasz felt his torn buttock,
    the pain…intense,
losing the touch of reality in shock
    he lost his sense.

Past his comrades Tomasz jumped back,
    into the depths he returned.
the converging sharks did instantly attack,
    the bloodied ocean churned.

TR

Torpedoed

Owned by the Southern Pacific Company
    the Antilles was a 7,000-ton steamer,
in the Great War it was a troop transport,
    Daniel T. Ghent was its commander.

The Antilles deposited 2,000 doughboys,
    at Saint-Nazaire, France,
against the Kaiser Wilhelm's Germany
    the soldiers would take a stance.

There was a young first assistant engineer
    the second named Leonard Lee Rue,
radiomen were Ausburne and McMahon,
    all of the Antilles' crew.

On October 15, 1917 the Antilles
    reset sail on a convoy to Brest.
Three escorts and three transports
    comprised the convoy heading west.

The Henderson, Antilles and Willehad
    were the three transports.
The Corsair, Alcedo and Kanawha
    provided protection as escorts.

One escort was formally a yacht owned by
    J. Pierpont Morgan the millionaire.
Refitted with batteries and ready for battles
    became the escort named Corsair.

Wind created a boisterous sea
    the second day out from port,
reduction in speed delayed the convoy
    due to flooding decks of an escort.

Torpedoed – S. S. Antilles.

Torpedoed – First Assistant Engineer Leonard Lee Rue on Left.

Torpedoed – Doughboys on the Antilles, 1917.

Wind continued, the weather worsened,
    the beleaguered Kanawha needed to take care,
and when a gale threatened
    the escort returned to Saint-Nazaire.

The Corsair and Alcedo patrolled out front
    and westward the convoy did continue,
following behind were the Henderson, Antilles,
    with the Willehad at the end of the retinue.

A small fire erupted upon the Antilles
    on October 17 before the dawn.
while extinguishing the fire lights were turned on,
    to which a U-boat could be drawn.

Up onto deck went Rue the young engineer,
    about 6 o'clock seaward he and others did peer,
light was poor but the dawn was clear,
    a zigzag course the ship did steer.

Rue watched whitecaps tossed by moderate winds
    and inhaled the fresh sea air.
At 6:45 A.M. the Antilles zigged
    directly astern of the Corsair.

Something in the water Rue and others did discern,
    streaking forth…a torpedo!
No time to raise the alarm of concern,
    Rue knew he'd lose his crew below.

The torpedo exploded against the ship,
    ripped open the engine room.
The water quickly flooded in
    entrapping men in their tomb.

The explosion followed with a quiver,
    alarming the Antilles' Commander Ghent,
feeling the ship from stem to stern to shiver,
    he knew of disaster's advent.

Torpedoed – The Escort Corsair Dropping Depth Charges, 1917.

The Antilles immediately listed to port,
    the lookout lost his grip,
hurled out of his perch he struck
    a hatch atop the ship.

Neither engines could be stopped nor headway checked,
    cold water hit the boiler,
explosion erupted releasing ammonia gas
    killing all but one boiler.

Commander Ghent realized the Antilles was sinking,
    ordered his men to abandon then.
four of ten lifeboats were able to be lowered,
    quickly filled with crewmen.

It was time to abandon ship
    Radioman Ausburne suggested to McMahon.
Ausburne followed McMahon to the door,
    but Ausburne locked himself in alone.

To go save himself Ausburne told McMahon,
    who futilely tried reentering the room.
Ausburne planned to continue manning his station
    consigning himself to his doom.

Other ships had no indication the Antilles was hit,
    became witness to a surprising spectacle.
The Antilles veered starboard settling by stern,
    the bow rose up like a pinnacle.

The bow raised but for a moment,
    vertically aloft hung the Antilles,
within five minutes after being torpedoed
    it plunged beneath the seas.

The sinking Antilles created a suction,
    sucking Engineer Rue down...down...down.
Holding his breath...into the depths he sank,
    deep enough would cause him to drown.

Torpedoed –
Leonard Lee Rue on the Left Being Rescued by the Corsair, 1917.

Suddenly Rue felt the downward drag release,
    like a cork he shot up fast.
Popping up between two wooden spars
    he wrapped arms around the pieces of mast.

Amidst the smoke, dust and dirty whirlpools
    Rue held the spars tight.
Of boats, wreckage and struggling men
    Rue focused upon within sight.

The Wellehad turned to port
    due to the chaotic scene,
the Henderson turned to starboard
    with stacks making a smokescreen.

The Corsair and Alcedo returned,
    steaming at full speed,
to the scene of destruction and debris,
    to reach men in their need.

Lookouts watched for the U-boat
    from each approaching escort,
dropping depth charges into the sea
    against the sub in retort.

To the spot where the Antilles sank
    the Alcedo returned,
picked up the struggling survivors
    from the sea that churned.

The Corsair circled around the perimeter,
    it's crew demonstrated dutiful courage
by rescuing survivors from sorting amongst
    lifeboats and the wreckage.

Eventually the Corsair came to the young engineer,
    for 5 ½ hours he did float.
Rue was hoisted up from the cold sea
    onto the deck of the boat.

Engineer Rue suffered hearing loss
    in the sea's contest of strife,
also a cut upon his scalp
    but was fortunate to retain life.

Rescued enlisted men were assigned below deck
    to warm up next to the engines,
the officers like Ghent and Rue were
    to thaw out in upper deck cabins.

Extra dry clothing was distributed by crews
    of the Alcedo and Corsair.
The rescued were thankful for the generosity
    of the rescuing crew's care.

Seeing that nothing else could be done,
    concerning the torpedoed ship,
the Corsair and convoy reset course for Brest
    and continued on their trip.

Two hundred and thirty seven men
    had comprised the Antilles crew.
The Alcedo rescued one hundred and seventeen
    and of fifty the Corsair did rescue.

At Brest the convoy docked,
    debarked the young engineer.
Before the escorts left the port
    the rescued raised a cheer.

TR

July 4, 2006

Unconnected Call

As a failure analyst at an electronics company,
    in the PAL Lab one 2004 early summer morning
I performed external inspection on a computer chip,
    using a low power microscope where I was sitting.

My friend Bob came in and I noticed
    a disgusted look on his face.
I asked what had happened and Bob began
    to tell what took place.

Other analysts gathered around as Bob told
    his story as it did unfold,
he was headed to the Product Analysis Laboratory
    but then decided to visit the lavatory.

As Bob sat on the commode within a stall
    his cell phone rang with an incoming call.
Bob's phone was held in a holder on his belt,
    to grip the sleek device his fingers felt.

Bob raised the cell phone up from its clasp,
    suddenly it slipped from his grasp,
into the liquid filled bowl it dropped,
    hit the water's surface…kerplopped.

Bob moved to retrieve his cell phone,
    the toilet's sensor activated the auto flush,
the water swirled in the bowl with a loud noise,
    the contents disappeared in a rush.

Hearing the phone still ringing Bob was able
    from within the plumbing system after its fall,
but since the cell phone was unreachable
    it remained an unconnected call.

TR

223

December 14, 2006

Unconscious

Two of my best friends were Myles and Gary,
    I met them by working in the room of garbage
in the Jenkins cafeteria while a student worker,
    at West Virginia Wesleyan College.

Myles, Gary and I were part of a work-study program
    which provided financial assistance to us,
we were placed in the garbage room together
    during my sophomore year on campus.

Myles, Gary and I chose our specific duties,
    I cleaned off the food scraps, garbage and stacked,
Gary stacked plates, utensils, glasses, cups, etcetera
    and the dishwashing machine Myles packed.

Usually a crew of four was needed to keep pace
    in the garbage room which was a fast-actioned place,
but Myles, Gary and I kept up, operated quite efficiently
    unless it was extremely busy.

A group, including myself, would visit Myles and Gary,
    who shared a room in a dorm.
Being familiar with them sometimes I didn't bother
    knocking…into their room I'd just storm.

On December 14, 1973, Gary, a guy named Nate and I
    debated in Gary's room about the shooting of bobcats
…if they attacked pet dogs versus being endangered,
    I then went to my room to retrieve some facts.

In my room, I found the information I had about bobcats
    in which to continue the debate with Nate and Gary,
I was scheduled to work in the garbage room for Myles
    soon, so I headed back to Gary's room in a hurry.

Without knocking I thrust open their door swiftly…
    thud…against something the door collided,
Gary was seated; I then viewed Nate's prostrate form.
    Nate was knocked out I concluded.

Apparently Nate had been on his hands and knees,
    with his head towards the door.
I went and sat in a chair next to Gary,
    while Nate lay unconscious on the floor.

Gary and I conversed while we waited
    for Nate to regain consciousness.
Shortly…Nate stirred and regained his bearings,
    I apologized and asked for forgiveness.

"If you ever do that again I will slit your throat!"
    Nate threatened…he was not appeased.
I again apologized but was angrily rebuffed,
    now I was not pleased.

I was curious and attempted to ask Nate why
    he had been down on the floor,
but he was belligerent and did not share this info,
    the reason remained unknown evermore.

"You shouldn't have been on the floor
    behind the door," I chided Nate without restraint,
he remained angry; I briefly considered clobbering him,
    but then I had to depart due to time constraint.

Thereafter Nate and I tolerated each other
    through our mutual friendship with Gary,
eventually in time we became friendlier
    though I continued to remain wary.

TR

July 21, 1982

Uncoordinated Action

On the morning of August 23, 1970,
    I assisted kitchen detail
to disassemble our group's makeshift kitchen,
    to leave on our watery trail.

The canoes were lined out along the beach
    which the scouts had begun to fill.
The sun began to light across the lake,
    but here persisted a morning chill.

Pots and pans were washed fast,
    Brian and I stowed them as our gear,
since pots and pans were usually packed last
    Brian and I often paddled in the rear.

With a distance to paddle and rapids to shoot
    it was good to get an early start,
so Uncle Bill led the scouts across the lake
    and other canoes began to depart.

Across the lake Brian and I followed,
    the sun overtook us,
we paddled into a channel called the Festebert
    leaving behind Lac Farbus.

Sandy bars initially made depth shallow,
    then depth did allow slow flow,
shrubbery grew thick along the Festebert,
    winding its channel narrow.

Brian paddled the stern, I was bowman
    paddling on my right side.
In one of the two canoes accompanying us
    was Kris, the Assistant Trail Guide.

Upon rounding a bend...I saw
    ahead in the brush in view
movement of sporadic wing flapping
    of a crested bird of blue.

The kingfisher seemed injured in erratic flight,
    onto a thin branch it did alight.
"Wonder what will happen to him?" voiced I.
    Kris replied that it would die.

Three canoes with spectators watched that moment
    at the kingfisher on stage,
in its act it flittered blue movement,
    disappeared beyond the foliage.

I informed Brian I wished to urinate
    but there was no place to beach
so we paddled over along the shore
    where shrubbery was within reach.

Brian held brush as I rose up unsteadily,
    my right hand extricated my p__is
and while I urinated I gripped tightly
    some of the overhanging coppice.

For me to hold tight Brian expressed concern
    since it was then his turn,
I observed Kris' canoe slowly glide,
    stop along the Festebert's opposite side.

Kris's bowman Jeb rose up to piss,
    supporting from the stern sat Kris,
but the bow drifted outward unbalancing the scout,
    overboard he fell out.

Hands became visible clasping onto the gunwale,
    up came Jeb's head in a sputter.
I restrained laughing considering it could have been me,
    the air filled with Kris' laughter.

I glanced back at the third canoe,
    each scout set aside his paddle,
surprisingly… both stood up simultaneously
    with the canoe in the channel's middle.

One leaned downstream and urinated,
    the other copied in action uncoordinated
causing a downstream face forward tilt.
    Splash!...they spilt.

The canoe swamped upon being upset,
    while Jeb climbed in his dripping wet,
I chuckled amidst laughter that others vent
    over humor of this incident.

Instructing Brian and I to get underway,
    to assist the scouts Kris decided to stay
so to catch the group we paddled away
    anxious to shoot Pikitakijuan Rapids today.

TR

February 27, 1981

Wake Up Little Rosebud

Linda and Mary are sisters
    and at one time they shared the same room.
They'd share gossip, secrets and clothes,
    in winter or when flowers bloom.

Linda would be the first to arise
    and of the time she'd surmise.
She'd glance at Mary sleeping so fragile
    but when awake was lively and agile.

Linda would proceed to astir her sister,
    she'd come over and give Mary a shake,
"Wake up little rosebud,"
    greeting the younger sister awake.

TR

September 6, 1981

<u>Waterproof Watch</u>

In the summer of seventy-four
    a watch I sought to buy,
a factory salary enabled me
    to give expensive taste a try.

At the jewelry store I looked over
    the selection so sophisticated.
All the variations of watches
    made the choice complicated.

Watches were either shock proof or
    waterproof or dust proof or…
any combination of two of three above
    displayed in the store.

The cost of a watch was determined
    by the number of proofs one acquired,
upon questioning the salesman about prices
    the number of proofs I considered.

I was willing to afford only one,
    either the shock proof or waterproof facet.
After much deliberation I chose
    a watch's waterproof asset.

After arriving home my brother was rambunctious,
    Jim and I went out back to spar.
Karate kicks were thrown and dodged
    occasioned with a jar.

Jim reared for a kick,
    reflex made my body twist,
out his leg did flick,
    blocked by my wrist.

Too late I remembered…my watch,
the crystal fractured upon impact,
my watch was no longer waterproof
with the fracture as a fact.

TR

March 1, 1981

White Cat

Mary and I were returning from shopping
    on the Belvidere-Riverton Road.
Sunshine glared as I drove towards the Delaware,
    a station wagon was our transportation mode.

A white cat burst forth from the brush
    into the path of the right tire's tread.
The tire's impact did crush,
    on the macadam the white cat lay dead.

I braked the car to a stop and shifted into reverse,
    to inspect the scene with a glance.
"That looks just like my white cat Jenny," Mary said,
    the white cat showed a strong resemblance.

"Wouldn't it be weird if this was an omen,"
    in my mind I formed a picture,
"if Jenny was killed the same way today,"
    I did whimsically conjecture.

In late afternoon Mary and I drove Route 519,
    and as we approached the end of her lane
a white cat lay motionless on the road's edge,
    seen through the car's windowpane.

It was Jenny, who lay on her side,
    hit by a car she had died.

TR

232

July 4, 2005

Whole Milk or One Percent?

Mary, Cathy, Beth Ann, Dan and I,
    on April 17, 2005,
went to Dorothy's for lunch after church,
    only a short drive.

We are members of a small, quaint,
    country Baptist church,
and the year before our pastor left
    leaving us in a lurch.

Dorothy is on the pulpit committee
    helping to find a new reverend,
to screen through possible candidates
    that the Lord may send.

To Dorothy's a small church group
    came to congregate,
to interact with Pastor Fred and his wife,
    he's a potential pastoral candidate.

During dessert Pastor Fred held his cherry pie
    in front of Beth Ann's face.
"It's mine," he teasingly removed it repeatedly before
    putting it in his place.

After dessert Pastor Fred and I,
    along with Cathy and Beth Ann,
settled in the living room
    with fifteen year old Dan.

Pastor Fred boasted about making his parents penniless,
    as he tried to take control of their every cent.
After his father died he sold their home
    and into a nursing home his mother was sent.

233

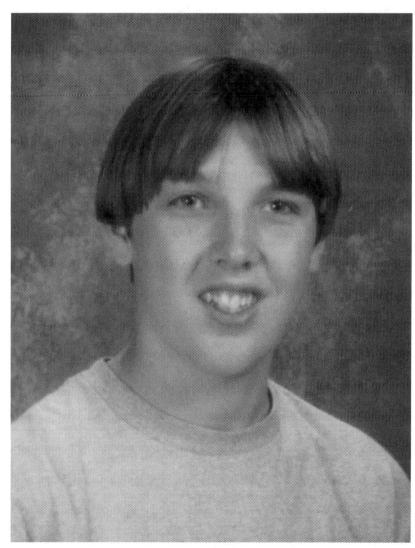

Whole Milk or One Percent – Dan Rue.

However there was a trust fund set up by his parents
    Pastor Fred explained.
And being in their name it is beyond his control,
    he bitterly complained.

With him lives his mentally slow sister,
    a retired Maryland state worker.
Pastor Fred proudly stated that he makes
    all of the decisions for his sister.

Dan leaned in towards the pastor
    to ask what he meant,
"Do you decide if she drinks
    whole milk or one percent?"

Pastor Fred stared expressionless
    as Dan tested his mettle,
eyes filled with surprise, anger, contempt…?
    Back Dan did settle.

Prior to our leaving Pastor Fred stood up,
    towards Dan's face he did poke
repeatedly with clenched fists,
    chuckled as it were a joke.

Later at home each offered their opinion
    about what Pastor Fred stood for,
when I asked Dan, he said,
    "The man has no sense of humor."

That evening Mary took a call from Dorothy,
    our opinion she did seek.
In the background of Mary I yelled,
    "He's a control freak."

Pastor Fred was not accepted
    as a pastoral candidate,
prayerfully a selection left in the
    Lord's hands of fate.

TR

November 28, 1982

<u>Winter's Approach</u>

Dawn has paled the gray sky,
    a cold front's force causes warmth to yield,
upon warming the car to go to work
    I have to scrape the windshield.

Leaves of red and yellow have browned,
    withered…dropped to the ground,
bare branches silhouette stoic statue shapes
    rooted across stilled landscapes.

Winter's approach lowers thermometers, raises thermostats,
    characteristic of a seasonal climate
to which all warm-blooded animals must acclimate,
    our goose down jackets help insulate.

With the advent of shorter days and frost
    comes increasing heating cost,
prompting usage of kerosene and wood for heat
    as cost alternatives to beat.

When adjoining to bed on these wintry evenings
    sheets and blankets are given a tug,
two bodies creating an addition of warmth
    can make both individuals quite snug.

TR

March 18, 1981

Wipeout in the Snow

Jim and I came to sleigh ride
    with the Jago clan at their homestead.
The Sunday had been bright with sunshine,
    we'd take turns descending by sled.

As a group we decided to make one last sleigh ride
    when darkness descended quite black.
I lay upon my stomach taking the lead
    with Mary upon my back.

We descended down through the snow,
    darkness made me unsure where to go,
cutting a corner too sharp…into the snow we did tumble,
    away from us our sled did ramble.

Jim approached and did see our figures loom,
    he veered off to the right to give us room,
into our sled he did collide,
    spilling into the snow he did slide.

Mary ran towards Jim to give assistance,
    striking Mary's ankle Bob's sled did toss,
a few feet into the air Mary did hurl
    landing upon her knee in the chaos.

Other figures followed through the darkness,
    in the lead was Mary's brother Phil.
He veered to the right striking a sled,
    into the snow Phil did spill.

Of Mary and I John did zip in-between,
    passing by quite near.
Mike avoided the chaotic scene,
    circling outwards he did steer clear.

We congregated…questioned…laughed
    upon finding everyone all right.
We deposited our sleds under the stoop's light,
    stepped into warmth from the night.

TR

September 12, 2005

<u>Worms Are Biting Me!</u>

Jake, a friend of mine from Sussex County,
    told me this tale
back in the late 1970s,
    hearing it made me pale.

One day in a man's backyard,
    he and a friend were talking,
and on the rocks along the property line
    his three-year-old son was playing.

While the father continued talking with his friend,
    his young son he could see,
when suddenly the boy cried out,
    "Daddy, the worms are biting me!"

The father and friend went over...horror!
    The nest of baby copperheads was numerous,
the son sat among them being bitten
    by the young reptiles so venomous.

The father grabbed up his son,
    rushed to his car parked near,
and drove rapidly towards the hospital,
    frantic for his son with fear.

Having been repeatedly bitten
    by many a baby copperhead,
before they reached the hospital
    the man's son was...dead.

TR

Worms Are Biting Me! – Copperhead.

March 15, 1981

Wounded Cape Buffalo

A wildlife photographer went to Zambia in 1970
    to visit a park named Kafue.
accompanying park officials on a cape buffalo hunt
    went the third named Leonard Lee Rue.

The park's native employees were paid in cape buffalo meat,
    each month the large herd would be cropped.
The park's professional hunters would go out
    and six cape buffalo would be shot.

On one hunt Len joined Robin,
    a park ranger and professional hunter.
Approaching the buffalo herd Len held a Hassalblad,
    guns were carried by Robin and a native partner.

Robin and his partner shot a couple.
    On one Robin aimed down the barrel's crest,
the cape buffalo was facing sideways.
    Robin shot it in the side of the chest.

The buffalo didn't even flinch but bled,
    turning into the brush it fled.
Robin had to follow to fulfill the hunting maxim
    that if you wound an animal you kill him.

Through the brush Len and Robin circled wide
    to get ahead of the buffalo shot in the side.
Robin carried a .375 H&H Magnum bolt action,
    he and Len proceeded with caution.

Scattered bushes 12' high and wide dotted the terrain,
    around one bush moved the ranger,
Len separated and proceeded around the other side
    and came face to face with the danger.

240

Wounded Cape Buffalo – Cape Buffalo.

The buffalo stood at a 75-foot distance,
    it had scented the men with its nose,
it had waited for them to advance
    with limiting their escape Len now knows.

Up the buffalo's head did fling,
    from each nostril blood squirted in a string.
With head erect the buffalo did charge
    approaching fast with its size so large.

Robin shot the buffalo in the neck,
    blood from the wound did spurt,
the bullet traveled through, out a hind leg
    but the buffalo came on as though not hurt.

Retreating behind the bush ran Len,
    passing him in back ran the warden,
ejecting a shell Robin did reload,
    continuing its charge the buffalo bore ill bode.

Len ducked, Robin whirled, fired over Len's head,
    the bullet struck in the forehead.
The buffalo collapsed scattering dust and gravel,
    at 10 feet distance it lay dead.

TR

November 8, 2005

Yellowjacket Sting

Mary, Cathy, Beth Ann, Dan and I
    attended a 1999 Labor Day party
as guests of the Franklin family,
    in suburban Alpha, New Jersey.

The Franklins entertained family and friends
    at their large home with a pool,
served hot dogs, hamburgers and accessories
    with ice packed soft drinks kept cool.

Yellowjacket wasps with half-inch blocky bodies,
    each armed with a barb less lance-like stinger,
abdomens banded in black and yellow…I was wary,
    around my soda can they did linger.

I raised my hamburger to take a bite,
    simultaneously a yellowjacket did alight,
felt a sharp stab as I was stung
    on the very tip of my tongue.

Even though I'm not allergic to bee and wasp stings,
    my tongue began to slowly swell,
a nurse of the Franklin family gave me medicine,
    attempting of the swelling to quell.

Despite the medicine that I had taken
    my tongue became increasingly swollen.
My speech became affected as my air way tightened,
    I began to become a tad frightened.

My swollen tongue was reminiscent to me
    of an increasing hoagie.
Mary decided to drive me to the hospital,
    haste was becoming vital.

Cathy, Beth Ann and Dan were occupied with swimming,
    to watch after them offered the Franklin family.
Quickly leaving Alpha to connect with Route 22,
    towards a local hospital drove Mary.

I could no longer talk due to being afflicted
    from the yellowjacket sting that inflicted,
the swelling tongue of my throat constricted,
    being able to breathe became restricted.

I determined that I could possibly die
    due to dwindling room for my palate
if treatment was delayed at the hospital
    because of having to fill out forms in triplicate.

We rushed into the reception room in emergency,
    Mary addressed the nurses on duty,
they took us into the back immediately,
    taking care of me quickly…thankfully.

I was placed in an angled chair on an incline
    and attached to me was an IV.
I felt reassured that now I'd be fine,
    Mary could see me resting comfortably.

Mary then followed the staff back to the reception area
    to fill out the paperwork that was necessary.
I was left to ponder the quick unfolding events,
    afterwards Mary relayed to me the rest of this story.

A nurse inquired, "I hate to ask you this
    but if your husband should die,
would you be willing to donate his organs?"
    Would Mary comply?

Knowing that I was out of danger due to the IV,
    and onto life I clung,
Mary responded to the expectant nurse,
    "Yes…and you can start with his tongue."

The nurses on duty were initially stunned
    at Mary's suggestion,
then burst into laughter
    releasing the pent-up tension.

TR

December 24, 2006

<u>Youthful Appearance</u>

I met my future wife Mary for the first time,
    when I came to the Jago place,
and I was a lanky boy of 17; she was 13.
    My…what a pretty face!

Mary had a round face, button nose, twinkling eyes,
    which reminded me of an angelic cherub,
I hid being attracted to her…her father Wes, a mechanic,
    was strong…of me I did not want him to drub.

It was in the late spring of 1994, when Mary was 36,
    of our children: Cathy was 7, Beth Ann 6, Dan 4,
there was a knocking…and with an investigation,
    a man was standing beyond the front screen door,

Mary, with her reddish-brown hair pulled into a ponytail,
    pushed open the screen door to meet this male.
The man looked at Mary, over her his eyes did roam,
    and inquired, "Is your Mommy at home?"

"I am the Mommy," replied Mary to the surprised man.
    Cathy, Beth Ann and Dan gathered around Mary,
to look at the man with curiosity, he then introduced
    himself as a salesman, somewhat tentatively.

The salesman began his sales pitch to Mary,
    but whatever he had to sell…she did not buy any.
When I arrived home, from working in a rubber laboratory,
    Mary related to me this humorous story.

Mary has always had a youthful appearance,
    with nary a wrinkle at age forty-eight,
and her skin is so soft; she uses minimal makeup,
    for her natural beauty there is no debate.

TR

December 16, 2006

Zilly Silly Songs by Dad

Cathy, Wathy, you're the one,
   who has so much fun,
Cathy, Wathy, we're especially fond of you,
   especially in fondue.
(Sung to Tune: Rubber Ducky)

Do you want a banana in your hand,
   or your hair Beth Ann,
do you want a banana in your hand,
   or your hair Beth Ann,
do you want a banana in your hand,
   or a banana in your hair,
do you want a banana in your hand,
   or your hair Beth Ann?
(Tune: If You're Happy and You Know Clap Your Hands)

Oh Beth Annigans, oh Beth Annigans,
   are you up to some shenanigans?
(Tune: Pomp and Circumstance)

Oh, Dan the Man was a rubber band
   he cooked his meat or
he cooked his feet,
   he cooked his stinking, smelly feeeeeet.
(Tune: Theme Music for the Beverly Hillbillies TV Show)

You are so beautiful to my knee, can't you see,
   you're everything I hoped for,
you're everything I need,
   you are so beautiful to my knee.
(For Mary: You Are So Beautiful To Me)

Handsome, fine Dad, asleep on the couch,
   he watches TV, but he's not a grouch. (My version)
                or
   he watches TV, but he is a grouch. (Kids' version)
(Sung to Tune: Little Bo Peep)

TR

247

Daniel Lewis Rue's Eagle Court of Honor – Dan Rue, 2007.

Daniel Lewis Rue's Eagle Court of Honor

An Eagle Court of Honor was held for Daniel Lewis Rue on Saturday evening of November 10, 2007, held at the Richmond United Methodist Church, Richmond, Pennsylvania. Daniel, son of Tim and Mary Rue of Lower Mount Bethel Township, became an Eagle Scout after his Board of Review on June 4, 2007. Daniel, a Boy Scout of Troop 14, within the Forks of the Delaware District of the Minsi Trails Council, Boy Scouts of America, had completed all of the requirements, including a project to benefit the community, needed to achieve the rank of Eagle. Daniel's Eagle project was a mobile challenge course for the Bangor Middle School.

Friends, mentors and scout leaders joined family to honor Daniel for his achievement. Jody Pysher, scoutmaster of Troop 102 of Bangor, was the Master of Ceremony, and presented the theme: History of the Eagle and Man. Troop 14 Scoutmaster Russ Hock led the Eagle Presentation. Assistant Scoutmaster Bill Bright gave the Eagle Charge, and former Scoutmaster Dave Johnson gave the Eagle Challenge. Donna Bright read the Legend of the Rose which honors mothers of Eagle Scouts and Matthew Bright presented roses to Mary Rue. Scout Chaplin Perry Morris recited the 23rd Psalm. Pastor Robert Rodriquez of Christ Baptist Church, Hainesburg, New Jersey, gave the invocation and benediction. Scout Leaders Jill Hock and Donna Bright were Greeters, Eagle Scouts Tyler Hughes and Nathan Pysher served as Daniel's Honor Guard, and Eagle Scout Billy Webb was an usher. Senior Patrol Leader Douglas Hock opened and closed the Court of Honor; Scout Jaron Hughes led the Pledge of Allegiance; and Scouts Wesley Hock and Justin Bright were included on the Color Guard.

Daniel Lewis Rue's Eagle Court of Honor –
Eagles Dan and Leonard Lee Rue III, 2007.

All of the Eagle Scouts in the audience were called forward and recognized. One of these was naturalist/wildlife photographer Dr. Leonard Lee Rue III, Daniel's grandfather. Stories of Daniel's scouting adventures were told and numerous letters of congratulations/certificates were presented. Jody Pysher presented to Daniel a special plaque commemorating his achievement, and Dr. William Horvath presented a certificate on behalf of the Bangor Area School District, to name just a couple. A reception following the ceremony was held in the church's banquet hall.

Philadelphia Urban Seminar – Cathy Rue, 2008.

Catherine Rue

Philadelphia Urban Seminar

On May 11, 2008, I travelled to Philadelphia to partake in a two week class called the Philadelphia Urban Seminar. This class was an opportunity for me to assist in an urban classroom by day, followed by evening seminars and one night of salsa dancing. A friend and I carpooled to La Salle University, where we would stay during our experience. We arrived on a beautiful, warm Sunday, which happened to be Mother's Day. Neither of us had been in Philly much and we were anxious, especially about finding the college. My anxiety steadily declined as I observed our surroundings. I was amazed at how calm the city felt. The majority of the men, women, and children were in their Sunday best and street vendors had assortments of gifts and gorgeous bouquets to entice pedestrians. I was pleasantly surprised at how many men were carrying flowers and little gifts for their loved ones.

When I signed up for the class, I was given the option of listing my grade preferences. I wrote down the grades, 1st-5th, attempting to avoid kindergarten. My professor assured us that we were very likely to get one of the grades we signed up for, but we would not know what school or classroom we would be assigned to until we arrived. To my dismay, I was assigned to kindergarten. Having worked with little children before, I felt that I might have gained the full experience by working with older children. My attitude quickly changed when I walked in the first day and discovered that I was in a bilingual class (one of the few in the program). I was excited to discover that I was in a class of 28 kindergarteners who were learning Spanish and English. Most of the students were of Puerto Rican or Dominican descent and most spoke primarily Spanish at home.

Unlike schools in suburban regions, these classroom teachers had smaller rooms, more students, and fewer supplies. Due to lack of space at the elementary school, my classroom, along with the four other kindergarten classes, were in one level of the Salvation Army building about two blocks from the elementary school. There was no administration staff and only one woman worked as a liaison between the two buildings. Overall, I think that the teachers liked the sense of freedom, but a negative to the separate building was that the kindergarteners had a full day from 8:20 a.m. to 2:45 p.m. and lacked a physical education program and recess. With the lack of movement, Ms. P, the classroom teacher, came up with short breaks throughout the day to help get out some energy.

Ms. P let me teach two of the English lessons and I understood 90-95% of the Spanish, which they spoke for a little more than half the day. Some students had trouble seeing the board and needed glasses. A few accidentally broke/lost theirs earlier in the school year and could not afford to buy new ones. The students in this class were taught the English and Spanish alphabet and how to use it, which meant they had twice the curriculum to learn. Sadly, even though most of them could form simple sentences in Spanish and English, Ms. P told me that only about 1/3 of the class was on target with the bilingual education, which will only increase in difficulty as they move up to first grade.

During our trip, we had a variety of experiences. My friends and I took the *Duck Tour*, which is a hilarious trip through old Philly, followed by sailing around Penn's Landing. The tour is on an amphibious duck, which is designed after the WWII DUKW vehicles to easily maneuver on land and sea. Each duck is tested by the U.S. Coast Guard and has a U.S. Coast Guard Certified Captain. Our tour was on a rainy day, which resulted in six tourists being on board: the four of us and one couple. We passed by Philadelphia's first post office, tavern, orphanage, and Black church (still owned by the Black community today), as well as South Street, where the first dance hall opened.

Our tour guide was satirical and enjoyed teasing my friend who was afraid of the water with playing the theme music from Titanic (as it sank). During the tour, our guide asked us who designed the U.S. flag. We did not know and he proceeded to tell us. He turned and said, "Do you know how I know this?" We did not. Proudly, he pointed to the building next to us and stated, "Well, it's right there on the plaque." As a class, we also received a personal tour of Philly from my professor who lives in Philly. She also took us to her very lively African-American church.

While most of trip was pleasant, we did have a few instances that were a little trying. Prior to our trip to La Salle, our professor warned us that in May the school may be hot, especially at night. Since it is an old school, there is no air conditioning, she advised us to bring fans. With this in mind, most of us brought fans and an assortment of clothing, mostly for warmer weather. Ironically, Philly was hit by a cold spell (mainly in the

50°Fs) during most of the two weeks and the campus heating system was programmed to be off until next September. At night we froze; I even used my towels and anything else I could rummage as extra blankets. To make matters worse, the water heater was extremely temperamental and the majority of our showers turned icy cold within two minutes. The last week we had a lice outbreak in the classroom next to mine. As a result, another college student from the neighboring kindergarten class and I bonded over Rid-X and cold water from the sink.

On Saturday, May 17, we had a community service day, where most of the Kutztown students cleaned the old Germantown Town Hall. Built in 1923, the town hall is gorgeous, but falling apart due to lack of use. It has been vacant since 1998, where it was used for city offices. Since then it has been added to the endangered properties list. It has marble pillars and a grand staircase that leads to the main floor, which is barricaded with a steel fence. I'm amazed that the city does not use this building for anything. In the back, we were dismayed to find a stream of trash leading to 2.5 feet of muck on the basement assess steps. The muck had formed due to trash piling up on the water drains. As an assembly line, we passed up the loads of wet, nasty trash. After a few hours, the floor could be seen again and the water began to recede. Sadly, I doubt it will stay that way. I hope that the historic building will be used again.

On our last Wednesday, May 21, we had an opportunity to take a salsa class. I love to dance and I had been looking forward to taking the lesson since I signed up for the class. The choreographer was charismatic and knew how to quickly and easily teach us the moves. Prior to that day, I hoped to dance with at least one man, just one. After the lessons, we had some time to practice. An older gentleman, like that of a friend's grandfather, came up to me and asked to dance. I accepted and during our first dance he frequently spun me around the room. I thought I might have been frustrating to him, but I smiled and he asked me to dance the second song. Thankfully, it was the meringue, which I "know" to some extent. After the dances were over, he commented that I was a good dancer, which was a great compliment as he was excellent. I did not get to dance with any other men during this time, but it was awesome.

The main reason that I volunteered for this opportunity was that I am in elementary education and wanted to experience city teaching. I loved the opportunity to help the students and speak with them in Spanish and English. Seeing the children's eyes light up when they grasped a concept is one of the most exciting feelings. The students were amazing. On my last day Friday, May 23, I was heartbroken to have to leave them. As the students were getting in line to leave, they were all giving me hugs. One student, who was always rolling around during class and barely listened to directions, told me she had a gift for me. She began to rummage through her book bag. I could see that we were about to leave and I assumed that the gift was probably a drawing with my name, Miss Rute (they had a hard time with Rue). At last, she found it, and handed me her school picture. I was deeply touched and told her, "Que bonita." (Which means, "How pretty"). She sheepishly smiled, hugged me and left with her class. I am truly blessed to have been able to partake in this experience and will cherish the memories.

Beth Ann Rue
Spring 2008

Road Trip Down South

Sight:

I remember the first time I had the epiphany. I had been walking through Wal-Mart that day in search of the movie *Dead Poets Society*. I thought it would be an easy find, but I was wrong. What turned into disappointment quickly became a new emotion, one involving curiosity and excitement. There I saw it. I had never seen this random movie, I had never heard of the movie, in fact, I knew nothing about it nor why I was drawn to it, but I couldn't stop walking past it. Every time my eyes scanned the shelves they would fall to the movie cover. After enough pacing back and forth, I grabbed it and bought it. It was necessary. It was fate. The fate brought forth through what can be seen.

The movie is titled *Into the Wild* and it is based on a true life story of a young man who in the 1990's traveled across America to find a worthwhile lifestyle. He was fed up with commercialism, materialism, and anything involving society. He went anyway he could to Alaska to live a liberated, domestic lifestyle in the Yukon Valley. It was the most beautiful passion I had ever seen in a human. Best part of it was that this man was real.

The Idea:

Upon watching that movie, my friends Jess, Hope and I started to discuss the wonders of road trips and traveling. It was then a farcical idea, one not to be taken seriously, but we could not be underestimated, for ideas bloomed into plans, and plans into more plans. Hope was basically my right wing. She and I grabbed this sucker of a dream by the balls and would not let go. It was a joke, but once we looked at each other and with the conversation that was something like, "Hope, I'm not kidding, I really want to travel America. I want to go away," and Hope said, "Ok, let's do it"...then it happened.

The Plans:

It was hard choosing the destination route, but we knew we'd only have five days max to work with. The main areas of interest were Nashville, Tennessee; Atlanta, Georgia; New Orleans, Louisiana, and somewhere in Florida. We wanted it to be a group of people, at the most: two cars and around seven or eight people. Many were invited and many were unable to come, but it worked out perfectly.

The group ended up involving Jess Reed, my friend through living together. Our years had been rough ones and our lives too. This was a good way to bring it home with a smile before I would move away. Also included was Chris, who's been Jess's boyfriend for more than a year. Hope Kincaid, the right wing in destruction and construction, was a huge ingredient. She has become an extremely integral part of my life and her undying passion for this trip made sure it was taken seriously. Lastly, there was me. I wanted this so bad... Experience is a lot of what life's about. You only speak of things because you know them and once you know them they can't be unknown. As far as I'm concerned, this trip was needed for my experience. I'll be the first to admit I don't know enough with my own mind and eyes. That is I didn't, and I still don't, but I certainly know more about the people that create this eastern side of America.

The Trip:

We planned our trip in less than two months. We planned for five days from Friday, May 23rd, 2008 to Wednesday, May 28th. We would leave early morning and get back whatever time we could on Wednesday. The important destinations mentioned earlier we visited except we scratched off Atlanta, Georgia, and never did go through Kentucky, not that that was a huge component, but I just like the name of that state and always thought it would be cool to say I was there.

The trip in total cost all of us put together only a little more than $400 for all five days. We traveled in my non-working-air-conditioned car (Electra is her name), and traveled on the road anywhere from 52 to 55 hours. We traveled so many miles, but I stopped looking at my mileage for fear that there was an early limit.

Road Trip Down South – Beth Ann Rue and Hope Kincaid, 2008.

Day 1: Taste and Feel:

We started off an hour late but it didn't take us long to make good progress. By lunch time we were in West Virginia making our way to some scenic area to eat. With neither much time on our hands nor patience for pretty greenery, we settled for some large parking lot straight across from a judicial center. We literally unpacked our giant cooler and food box and began our picnic lunch with sandwiches on the car. It was weird, it was not all that extravagant, but it was certainly a new experience.

By later in the day, we grew tired of driving again, but this time our food destination was one that I had been only dreaming of: the one and only Sonic. We hit one up in southern Virginia, and let me tell you, the commercials do not lie about their drinks.

Finally, we reached Tennessee. Before it grew dark we embarked upon a gas station, although I don't believe it was to get gas. When there, we knew we were in another culture, because the car that pulled up next to us seemed to have no inside cover on the door in the passenger seat and apparently the door in the driver's seat was jacked up too, because the driver refused to open it and kept jumping in and out of the window. It was humorous, but it was just weird too.

By nighttime, specifically 10:00 p.m., we finally reached Nashville, Tennessee, with no plans of where to go once there or where to sleep. We grabbed the first best offer we could find at a Best Western in their Honeymoon suit. They supplied us a discount offer of $150 when it would usually be about $250 per night. We knew we were hitting gold and unbelievability (I'm pretty sure I just made up that word). The night, however, did not end there. We went on to the town, in the watery streets (due to Tennessee's freak-show hard rain) and found our way to the busy section. We saw crowded sidewalks with ages of early 20's to late 40's people socializing and making their way to bars, food, and more people.

Just when we were thinking of heading back, the great eyes of fate found us a limo and a free ride to a disco club in another part of town. No lie, we were just walking and approached by a sweet southerner willing to give us transportation and free passes to this new club called Disco Hollywood, or something of that sort. Of course, it sounded too good to be true, but we bagged the opportunity and it was quite a sight. The club had Saturday Night Fever flashing floors and the people were dancing to 70's beats (including the gentleman). It was unbelievable. To finish off the night we headed back to our luxury room, chilled in the hot tub for a good while, and made wonderful sleep in our King Size bed. Yes, all four of us in one bed.

Day 2: Joys of Pain and Mystery:

To preserve and make the most of our day in Nashville, we got up fairly early, ate a Best Western styled breakfast, went to Tennessee's visitor infested Parthenon, and also found time to put new holes in our bodies. We found this piercing store that seemed legitimately valid and I received another notch in my left ear while Jess let them pierce her navel. It was a good midday event before we once again did a picnic parking lot.

The day quickly moved forward for the real rush, the journey to New Orleans. An epiphany was presented to us as we traveled through Alabama and into Mississippi. That realization was that we were most excited about our next stop. However, dinner had to slow us down, dinner at the infamous Cracker Barrel while still in Mississippi. Let me tell you, it was the first real meal we had on the trip, and my stomach couldn't handle it. By the time I was halfway through my steak I realized I had wasted my money. Upon paying I quickly proceeded to the toilet and filled each flush with a mouthful (literally).

Mississippi was also full of other adventures, like the creepy, isolated gas stations off the highway, or the overly friendly people (this included cat calling from cars) at every sight. I kept thinking I should know some of these people.

The day was completed with an exhausting introduction to the loud New Orleans. We somehow entered at midnight in the most crowded section of town, but it was the energy level we were looking for. Our excitement quickly turned into serious trouble when getting a bit lost while looking for something we hadn't planned out too fully. All was well and good when we managed to get to our Hotel outside of the city and by then, we at least had a better understanding of the city.

Day 3: Unique Is Feeling New Again:

New Orleans was amazing. We began our new morning by taking a Ferry Ride to the French Quarter area where we went to an aquarium (the first one I had ever been to) and then went for a walk about the town. The devastation Katrina had caused a couple years back was barely noticeable. The buildings created a European city feel with second floor balconies.

The streets are small and along the sidewalks we would find street performers: the mimes, the clowns, the robots, the artists, the gypsies, psychics, palm readers, painters, and etc...one word: new. I've never seen anything quite like it. We went to this one restaurant although I do not remember the name, but it was located on Bourbon St., known well for its significance in Mardi Gras. I had an alligator Po Boy which is their term for sandwich. The accents are different there, but not just southern, just different altogether. They get mad if you say New Orleans by saying it like leans as in leaning, instead of 'Orlins' that rhymes with fins, which I found out from a laugh by my waiter due to my pronunciation. Leaving there was not easy, but it had to be done as we ventured to Lakeland, Florida.

We had to travel back up to the Gulf and through both Mississippi and Alabama again just to get to Florida. Once reaching the sunshine state we found ourselves some burgers at Hardees, a fast food place better known down south. We didn't get to Florida till 3am, and once we did, somehow Hope and I stayed up for a movie and then readily enjoyed sleep time. If I could do it again, I would cut out the movie cause it was a terrible independent horror film; absolutely terrible.

Day 4: Hearing Sounds We Shouldn't:

Monday was the first time we slept in, our day was shorter due to this. We went to IHOP, where Jack, my friend and host of our stay in Florida, was currently employed. Then we made our way on a tour around Jack's school called Florida Southern. It is known well for its Frank Lloyd Wright architecture, so it was a good school to be given a tour. We ended our tour at the dock of Lake Hollingsworth. The Lake is almost a perfect circle 3 miles around and about 1.5 to 2 miles across. Unbeknownst to us, upon entry and enjoyment in the lake, it is full of God's marvels like alligator and water moccasins. Somehow the sounds below my belly as Hope, Ted (Jack's roommate) and I swam across the waters didn't stop me from making it all the way across. I did not know what the sounds were. I think I was more scared of drowning at some random point in the middle than what lay beneath me. Needless to say, we were so proud of ourselves. We actually swam across a lake.

That night, we had a barbecue at Jack's place and played games with friends. It wasn't as much action as we had gotten used to in the previous parts of our trip, but it was certainly necessary to our skin and bones.

Day 5: Home Is in Your Soul and Apparently Up North:

When we left, we decided to make a fairly straight line up Highway 95. The few stops along the way on that Tuesday involved driving through Disney World where we visited the downtown area and just took in the surroundings. Not a lot was to be seen, but it was certainly nice to witness where Disney actually is as it had always been part of my childhood imagination. We also stopped in St. Augustine, Florida which was founded by the Spanish in 1565 and also has a beach with the weirdest feeling sand I had ever felt and the warmest ocean compared to our northern icicle waters. The sun did not seem as burningly hot as expected, but it could have been because we were only there for 2-3 hours before we left for food at the only chick fillet I've ever seen outside the Lehigh Valley Mall.

When we finally embarked into the Peach State, also known as Georgia, we decided to make one stop in Savannah before it got dark. We were there for a few hours just sight-seeing and taking in the town. It's honestly more of an old folks vacation area, especially with all its Civil War history, but I'm glad we added another destination to our "I've seen here____" T-Shirts (which we never really purchased, but I just made up for overly exaggerative effect).

We somehow managed to drive through the night and make it to South Carolina, pass South of the Border, and North Carolina before Day 6 arose. While in North Carolina, we made one stop at this gas station that somehow was the busiest gas station at 11pm at night. It entailed surprisingly good coffee, almost no Caucasian individuals, and van loads of what would appear to be Latino looking individuals, probably more than should fit in any van-sized vehicle. Needless to say, we felt a bit out of place. The culture of America will never cease to amaze me, and neither will the amount of people you can fit into a moving van.

Day 7: A Drive, A Realization, An Epiphany If You Will:

I was designated to drive for it was more than well my time to do so. As my hands were holding the steering wheel and my eyes were gazed at the road, it was nothing but semi-flat steering, darkness, and repetition. I'm fairly certain the clock read some ungodly a.m. hour like two or three but even though in my daily life those hours are part of my awake life, in driving land, that is my time to shed some sleep. I could not handle it, so until we reached Baltimore, Maryland, Chris stayed at the wheel so I could get some healthy shut eye and not be in the position to create four coffins.

We reached Baltimore at sixish a.m. It was suddenly cold for the first time on our trip. We walked the Lower Harbor area and found our way to Panera Bread in the morning where we enjoyed city coffee, saw the craziest inside jungle mall, and then we realized we didn't want to stay in the Baltimore area for much longer. Somehow we got lost. Again. And again. And it seemed like we were lost for a good hour until I found someone at a gas station that actually knew English, and could get us on our way. We kept going onward until we reached the Philadelphia area and decided to make one last stop at the King of Prussia Mall where I had never been prior to the road trip. We delayed there, bought some things, and made it back to Bethlehem at 1 p.m. Our last moments together were there at Franks Italian Pizza on 191. We discussed our trip, the best and the worst, the unbelievability of it all, and we said our goodbyes. Not goodbye like, "bye, I'll never see you again," but more like "bye to an experience that won't be had by most and may not be embarked on by us again." It was a sad goodbye. It was a hard goodbye. But it was a goodbye to one of the most amazing experiences of my life.

We are meant to journey to learn. New experiences create a more accurate reality to understand not only who others are, but who you are. I hope to further my understanding of this world we live in. Thank you for letting me share my new point of view with you.

Mary Rue
June 21, 2009

Mary's Love Letter

Dear Tim,

I love you. I am glad that we are married after we fell in love so many years ago. You are an excellent provider for our family, and have given an excellent example of work ethics to our children.

Life has certainly had its joys and sorrows. I'm glad that we have been together to share the good times with my family when my parents were alive, and that you treasured the time with them as much as I. They loved you, too, as a son.

I am happy that you were there with me in dealing with the difficult trials of my sister Kathy's cancer and death. You were special in her eyes and she wanted you to take care of me! (Amazing girl!) She saw something special in us as a couple.

You were with me during my folks' good days and bad. We desperately wanted for them to thrive, not die. They could have been such a blessing with all the grandchildren. We all missed out. You saw my childhood family as a blessing, "Walton-like", despite our frailties. You were a part of us; we enjoyed bringing you into the mob. Life was difficult yet full of love for one another. You were a witness to love, and shared with us in our daily, hectic lives.

I remember serenading you and how you loved it. I remember our long walks up the mountain, holding hands, casually conversing, sharing our hopes and dreams, getting to care deeply for one another and our families, dreaming of our future together??

I was there for your grandma Castner's funeral after she died, even though we were having difficulty. Your Gram Castner loved me, and wanted you to marry me. Wise woman! She also saw something special in us as a couple. Her passing brought us back together to work things out instead of splitting up forever. We belonged together.

After we married, I longed for children. Miscarriage. I was devastated; you brought comfort into the hospital with a teddy bear! How cute! Our first child is in Heaven, waiting for the rest of us to come home. Steven? We'll know when we get there.

Children brought us great joy. Sorrow came with my folks' deaths. I missed them terribly, and so did you. I longed for touching them, seeing them, hearing my Dad's raucous laughter, my mother's lilting voice, seeing them disappear upstairs...there was an emptiness in my heart without them. I clung to memories of their voices, cried when I saw their pictures late at night, longing for them.

Praise God for different mentors in my life who helped fill in the gap after my folks died, parent figures such as Kathy More, who have offered their love and affection and time to share.

I praise God that you and I worked out our struggles through difficult years while our children were still home. We still loved and cared for one another, and saw the bigger picture of how we could selfishly destroy our children if we devoured one another in our struggles. Our kids witnessed our battles, but also the beauty of being one flesh.

I praise God that you were (and are) involved in the ongoing process of mentoring our children. Teen years were especially a challenge, but we were there for our children, and for one another. We rejoiced in one another's joys and helped each other in times of sorrow. "Rejoice with them that do rejoice, and weep with them that weep." Romans 12:15.

I praise God that we do love one another, despite conflict, pain, or sorrow. We are there for one another, and care for one another. Life is too difficult without one another's support. I pray God will increase our passion for one another, to glorify Him, and bring us joy.

"Charity suffereth long, and is kind;
charity envieth not;
charity vaunteth not itself,
is not puffed up,
Doth not behave itself unseemly,
seeketh not her own,
is not easily provoked,
thinketh no evil;
Rejoices not in iniquity,
but rejoiceth in the truth;
Beareth all things,
believeth all things,
hopeth all things,
endureth all things.

Charity never faileth..." I Corinthians 13:4-8
    Tim, I love you. We <u>belong</u> together. I praise God for you.
    Happy Father's Day!
    Your wife, Mary

Genealogy Chart

Genealogy Chart

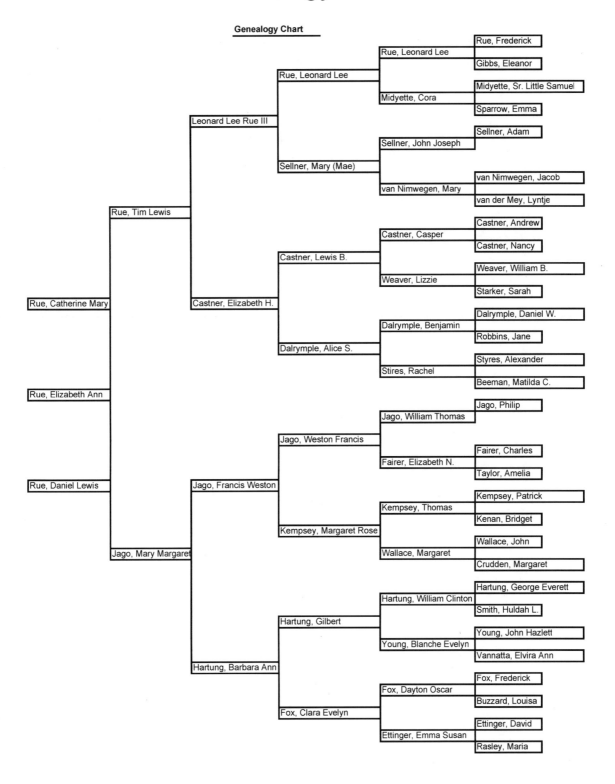

				Rue, Frederick
			Rue, Leonard Lee	
		Rue, Leonard Lee		Gibbs, Eleanor
			Midyette, Cora	Midyette, Sr. Little Samuel
	Leonard Lee Rue III			Sparrow, Emma
				Sellner, Adam
		Sellner, Mary (Mae)	Sellner, John Joseph	
				van Nimwegen, Jacob
Rue, Tim Lewis			van Nimwegen, Mary	
				van der Mey, Lyntje
				Castner, Andrew
		Castner, Lewis B.	Castner, Casper	
				Castner, Nancy
			Weaver, Lizzie	Weaver, William B.
	Castner, Elizabeth H.			Starker, Sarah
				Dalrymple, Daniel W.
		Dalrymple, Alice S.	Dalrymple, Benjamin	
				Robbins, Jane
			Stires, Rachel	Styres, Alexander
Rue, Catherine Mary				Beeman, Matilda C.
				Jago, Philip
		Jago, Weston Francis	Jago, William Thomas	
				Fairer, Charles
			Fairer, Elizabeth N.	
Rue, Elizabeth Ann				Taylor, Amelia
	Jago, Francis Weston			Kempsey, Patrick
		Kempsey, Margaret Rose	Kempsey, Thomas	
				Kenan, Bridget
			Wallace, Margaret	Wallace, John
Rue, Daniel Lewis				Crudden, Margaret
				Hartung, George Everett
		Hartung, Gilbert	Hartung, William Clinton	
				Smith, Huldah L.
			Young, Blanche Evelyn	Young, John Hazlett
Jago, Mary Margaret				Vannatta, Elvira Ann
	Hartung, Barbara Ann			Fox, Frederick
		Fox, Clara Evelyn	Fox, Dayton Oscar	
				Buzzard, Louisa
			Ettinger, Emma Susan	Ettinger, David
				Rasley, Maria

About the Author

Tim Lewis Rue was born August 5, 1954 at Monroe Hospital in East Stroudsburg, Pennsylvania but raised in Pahaquarry Township, Warren County, above the Delaware Water Gap, on the New Jersey side of the Delaware River. At the age of 15 Tim moved to Belvidere, New Jersey; he graduated from Belvidere High School in 1972. He graduated from West Virginia Wesleyan College in 1976 with a Bachelor of Science degree in biology. Tim has worked as a laboratory technician. Tim married Mary Margaret Jago from Harmony Township, Warren County, New Jersey in 1981. Tim and Mary moved across the Delaware River and raised three children: Catherine Mary, Elizabeth Ann and Daniel Lewis in Lower Mount Bethel Township, Northampton County, Pennsylvania.

The author's interest in history and genealogy led to articles being published in The Warren County Companion magazine in the early 1990s. Tim wrote a newspaper series in 1995 entitled *Where Were You When World War II Ended*, commemorating the 50th anniversary of the war's end. Friends and relatives were interviewed about their wartime experiences for this series. Tim coached Lower Mount Bethel soccer teams in the late 1990s. He served as a merit badge counselor starting in 2002, then for a period of time as an Assistant Scout Master for the Boy Scouts of America.